Girl Forgotten

CARLA ACHESON

This Paperback Edition First Published by Charlotte Greene, Dorset England, 2017.

Printed in the United Kingdom, or country of purchase.

This book is a work of fiction. Names, characters, places and events are used fictitiously.

ISBN PRINT: 978-1910711149
EPUB: 978-1910711156

FIND OUT MORE ABOUT THE AUTHOR AT
www.carla-acheson.com

Dedicated to all children who have ever felt unloved.

Word by word we come
To lay a story in your lap
Are you surprised?
Will you like it?
Now it is yours...
A story called life

"Yes. Forever and always," said Mama.
"No matter where you are, no matter how big you grow.
My heart will never, EVER let you go."

I'll Never Let you Go - Marianne Richmond

One

Greenwich, London 1905

Annie

I watched the carriage disappear into the grey mist before walking towards the building. A knot of apprehension coiled around my stomach as I viewed the peculiar way the shadows spread across the ground. It was an unwelcoming sight, and one that I imagined might well deter visitors from entering.

The orphanage had been erected more than four centuries ago. I learned that it was once a monastery for a Sistine order of monks and used as a sanctuary during times of hardship and war, offering immunity to persons persecuted by acts of injustice. I could tell that it held many stories untold, and yet I could not help but think it appeared strangely unbalanced, for despite its gloomy exterior the gardens surrounding it appeared attractive and well kept.

The gravelled stones crunched loudly beneath my shoes. I raised my head, straightened my shoulders and inhaled a deep breath. Stepping up to the entrance I knocked three times on the door and waited a good many moments until I heard the sound of footsteps approaching.

An elderly woman with stooping shoulders opened a small window within the main door and peered at me with narrowed eyes.

'Who are you?' she enquired.

'Miss Annie Reinhart. I believe that Mrs Stradlin is expecting me?'

She raised an eyebrow. 'Mrs Stradlin is away. What is your business here?'

'I received a letter from her.' I retrieved the note from my purse and handed it to her directly. 'We are to meet this very morning.'

The old woman stared at it for a moment and I wondered whether she was able to read the words on the page. I half expected her to close the door shut but instead she unbolted a heavy latch and stood to one side.

'I will fetch her assistant Miss De Bours in her absence.'

I nodded gratefully and stepped into a hallway which had been lit with candles placed high up on shelves; away from small fingers I surmised. I felt unsettled in the unfamiliar setting, though I was certain there was no particular cause.

'Please be seated,' she instructed me before departing.

A pungent scent of beeswax reached my senses as I sat down on a hard wooden bench where the faint sound of children's voices filtered down a giant staircase opposite me. They were singing some kind of a hymn and the sound was pleasant to my ears, reminding me that within these concrete walls blood of my blood had once lived and breathed.

It was hard to fathom.

My muscles began to ease from their tension and I closed my eyes to concentrate on the sound which seemed to transform into a heavenly choir, but my reverie was soon cut off when I heard footsteps approach.

A slim young lady stopped before me. She wore her dark hair neatly tied at the nape of her neck except for a few stray strands which fell lazily over one eye, a high necked blouse, and a long crinoline skirt that narrowed at the waist.

She greeted me warmly.

'Miss Reinhart, how lovely to meet you, I am Miss De Bours. I must apologise on behalf of my benefactor Mrs Stradlin, she had some pressing business to attend to in the north of the city. I am afraid I have a very busy day ahead attending to her duties. I had planned to sit with you for a formal introduction but would you mind terribly if we talked whilst visiting some of the children?'

I nodded politely, hiding my disappointment that I would not acquire the opportunity to sit with her and ask about my sister, though I had mentioned in my initial correspondence that I would like to be acquainted with the orphans too. I had lain awake the previous night wondering what they looked like.

How did they behave?

Were they the same as the urchins that cowered in the street corners of the more run-down cities, begging for a crumb? Or were these children better groomed, maybe even given an identity that might afford them some hope of a future.

Miss De Bours cut into my thoughts.

'I did manage to source a folder with some minor content relating to your sister which you may like to take for your own perusal, though I must ask that it be returned to us.'

She handed me a thin folder and I accepted it from her gratefully, then together we walked on as she spoke about the daily affairs at the orphanage.

Despite it's gloomy interior I was impressed by its sheer size and well polished floors, a direct contrast to the grubby windows which had greeted me on arrival.

After she had showed me a few of the common rooms where the children normally gathered each day to indulge in various tasks and activities, we reached the top of the staircase where a shuffling sound could be heard. I froze at the highest step to witness a great gathering of orphans standing patiently at the entrance to a large wooden door.

'This is the dining hall. The children are about to consume their luncheon Miss Reinhart, you may sit with us quietly and watch.'

I thanked her, feeling the gaze of many pairs of eyes studying me curiously. I offered a warm smile to one young boy, but his eyes nervously darted away.

'Do they receive many visitors?' I enquired.

'It is rare that the children receive any visitor at all,' she said matter-of-factly. 'On public holidays a few of the local dignitaries and persons from charitable societies might arrive for an informal visit, but other than that I am afraid they do not see the outside world or any of those who occupy it.'

The news saddened me. I could not begin to imagine the number of souls to have perished here over the years, with the orphanage being their entire and only existence.

I took note of their appearance. It was a mix of gender ranging from seven to twelve years. The males appeared much more shoddy and unkempt than the females in their grey smocks, with many wearing torn breeches and ragged shirts. Most were barefoot, and those that were fortunate enough to possess footwear revealed blackened toes which peeped through small frayed holes.

I sensed a lack of excitement or frivolity that one might expect from a crowd of children, but nevertheless, I joined them as the doors opened wide and we all flooded into a large hall where the stench of over-boiled vegetables assailed my nostrils and I rudely had to cover my nose with my handkerchief.

Two long tables were positioned alongside one end of the room taking up nearly the entire length of the wall with various persons stationed behind it. Hot steam rose from large steel vats and beside that sat a stack of wooden bowls, spoons and cups.

Miss De Bours instructed me to seat myself in a corner and I did as she asked, hoping that I might somehow blend into the sombre grey concrete wall and not draw attention to myself. Thankfully it seemed the children were all too hungry to be particularly concerned with my presence. They began to move steadily in a line, each taking up a spoon, cup and bowl into which the food was ladled as they shuffled along.

Lastly, they selected an apple from a barrel at the end and quietly seated themselves on the hard benches, each seeming to have a designated place appointed to them. I took note of how the girls sat on a separate table opposite the boys keeping their eyes focused away.

A child giggled causing others to follow suit.

'Silence!' bellowed a gentleman striding into the room with a limp so pronounced I was immediately concerned that he would trip and fall. I stifled an impolite giggle at his stature, though his voice more than compensated for the lack of a physical presence. He was barely taller than the oldest child in the room. He hobbled along on a short cane, stopping here and there to observe the children's behaviour.

'Eat and be silent,' he remonstrated.

'That is Mr O'Brady, the gentleman in charge of the dining period,' said Miss De Bours. 'He is a man of honourable upstanding and has long served our humble institution, though he is very soon ready to retire.'

Finally, when all the children were occupied with their luncheon, Mr O'Brady sat on a bench alongside a handful of ladies who I presumed to be assistants and cooks. They chattered to each other and seemed cheerfully engaged in their own affairs. It was not the foreboding scene I had envisaged in my mind, but rather a well organised sanctuary for the unwanted orphans. I did, however, have to remind myself that the orphanage might have been very different twenty-five years ago.

Miss De Bours smiled at me as I took in my surroundings.

'Here we only attend to the older children, we do not mix young with old as you can imagine what a dreadful commotion might ensue otherwise. The younger children are fed in separate quarters by different carers.'

'Would this be the typical fare that they receive?' I asked impertinently, careful not to mention how the mere sight of it spoiled my appetite to a very large degree.

'Today it is a mix of ground vegetables and potato pairings. If you were to consider the vast amount of mouths we are required to feed daily Miss Reinhart, you will see that we are doing our utmost to ensure there are enough provisions. On rare occasions we may include a morsel of fat or bacon.'

I nodded. How could I expect an establishment such as this to be any different? It was, at the very least, preventing the children from succumbing to starvation, but in truth the pallor of their skin, sunken eyes and subdued manner could easily have revealed such a poor quality diet.

My thoughts returned to Pixie and I wondered if this was the sort of gruel she would have consumed during her time here. I felt wretched even to think of it. That my parents and I would each morning consistently dine on fresh produce, eggs, bread, crumpets and fruit, when she was quite possibly digesting a mixture of unpalatable gruel. I felt an unwelcome anger suddenly rise up within me and tried hard to quell it.

The seating arrangements within the dining hall intrigued me. There appeared to be a small group of adult staff compared to such a large amount of children. I looked around paying close attention to the setting wondering where Pixie would have been placed if she was incapable of feeding herself and in need of assistance. She most likely would have been attended to personally.

I fidgeted in my chair, feeling suddenly laden with so many questions that I felt an irrational urge to stand up and shout them all aloud at once.

In truth, I held only a few facts about my sister. I had not probed into her life at the orphanage to avoid a bitter reaction from my parents. Both tended to avoid any discussion on the matter. Mother, particularly, would become deeply upset and obstinate whenever I tried to talk about her, and if I persisted she would begin to suffer from a nervous bout of hysteria that would spoil our entire afternoon, or at worse - the entire week!

I also did not wish to provoke hostility from my fiancée Matthew, who with all intents and purposes believed that any matters involving the deceased should never be disclosed unless some covert or indiscreet monetary affair was associated with them. A viewpoint which I attributed entirely to his occupation within the financial industry.

My parents sent Pixie away from our family home at the age of five years after she suffered a dreadfully debilitating accident. I was twenty years of age when I accidentally discovered that she had been brought to this orphanage upon being presumed incumbent with a spinal injury. I also learned that she perished just a year later. I knew nothing about her short life here and possess only a faded image of her which lives on in my memory.

The sound of heavy chair legs being dragged across the floor resounded across the room as the children all stood in unison to the blow of a whistle. Mr O'Brady took a few minutes to stand to his feet, finally aided by a robust woman at his side. The children waited patiently. He then waved his arms in the air and directed them out of the hall in two lines.

One little boy stayed behind and leapt from bowl to bowl to scoop up the remains, pushing them into his mouth greedily until the gentleman blew his whistle loudly and he jumped back into line.

'Greed will not be tolerated here,' he told the boy sternly.

Miss De Bours led me out of the hall where I consulted my watch and saw that there was yet one more hour remaining before my carriage was due to return.

During this time she showed me the different rooms within the orphanage. It all appeared very dull and lacking in colour with its wide hallways, steep staircases and dusty wall hangings of unrecognisable individuals bearing sombre expressions. It seemed like a good many of the rooms were not put to the greatest efficiency, appearing to be locked shut with dusty wooden door knobs highlighting their lack of use.

'Would you like to visit the younger children?' Miss De Bours asked.

'Thank you, that would be lovely,' I replied.

I followed her up another curving flight of stairs and along a hallway with wide tall windows that stretched along the full length of the wall. Though they were grubby, the pale light pleasantly reflected the rolling green hills outside.

Finally, I was led to a room which seemed brighter than any other I had witnessed before, and inside were gathered a circle of ten or so infants, seemingly not older than four years of age. They seemed to be absorbed in an activity of chalking upon pieces of slate. One girl heavily pressed her chalk onto it defiantly whilst another paid close observance and attention to her task.

A middle-aged assistant wearing a white apron sat upon a chair beside the window. She appeared to be indulging in a sewing activity of some kind, and by her stance and expression alone I gauged that she might be the class of woman to possess a good degree of patience and kindness. One child sat contentedly by her skirt timidly sucking her thumb.

I noticed that each child's hair was tangled, and their faces and smocks stained with dirt and soot from the nearby hearth. One girl promptly stood to her feet and began to hop around the room raising her arms and jumping in delight whilst repeating in a high tone, 'We have not a single crust to feed you.'

'Why does she speak that way?' I enquired, alarmed by her actions.

Miss De Bours sighed. 'She repeats the words her mother or father might have said, Miss Reinhart. One thing we cannot do is erase the children's memories. They will often repeat some disturbing revelations. It is best to ignore many of these mumblings for fear that highlighting them might only cause anxiety and further repetition. Sooner or later they do cease.'

I watched as another girl with bonny auburn curls coiled tightly to her head jumped to her feet, ran to the window, and pointed outside. She then returned to my skirts and touched the material with her small fingers, her cherubic pink lips forming a playful pout.

I crouched down to face her.

'What is it you are trying to say little angel?' I asked with a smile.

She then clasped my finger inside her small hand and led me to the window.

'Sun,' she said pointing up at the sky.

'Yes,' I smiled. 'There is a sun in the sky.'

She nodded and raised both arms, a gesture for me to lift her.

'May I?' I asked.

Miss De Bours stood a few feet away appearing concerned.

'I would not advise it. If all the children are mollycoddled this way, how would we ever cope?'

I looked down at the little girl's innocent face which melted my heart so intensely that I became flushed and agitated.

The sound of wheels turning upon gravel alerted me to my carriage approaching the building.

'I must leave now but I will return again,' I told the little girl as I began to walk away.

Her face quickly spread into a mask of dissatisfaction and she pulled at my skirt with force, throwing herself against my leg.

'Miss Rebecca, go back to your drawing slate,' Miss De Bours commanded.

I had almost reached the door when the little girl burst into a fit of tears and became unexpectedly hysterical.

'Mama,' she burst openly in a fit of passion. 'Mama, please stay.'

My heart sank as I watched an assistant tear the girl away from my leg. Her imploring look showed deep distress and resentment as her crimson cheeks became a sopping mess of tears.

Miss De Bours took hold of my arm and urged me away. 'We must leave right now. It is for the best.'

The young girl's screams echoed along the hallway as I retreated, quickening my pace as my chest became heavy with each step. I feared that I should hurry or I would not be able to leave her.

'Why does she cry so passionately?' I asked.

'Miss Reinhart, these children have suffered greatly. Do not trouble yourself further with their plight, it is enough that the brave assistants here are required to do so.'

'Please. Explain her position to me,' I pleaded again.

She sighed and faced me directly. 'Very well. If you truly wish to hear it.'

'I do,' I replied bravely, though I knew the information would tug at my heart.

'Her mother was a prolific drinker. She abandoned her daughter into the street early one morning after a night of intoxication. It was fortunate enough that the child was found alive, for any kind of calamity could have fallen upon her.'

'But I am not her mother, why did she act as if I were?' We continued down the staircase towards the main entrance.

'No, you are not her mother, but you are a woman, and you have come from outside these very guarded grounds. The child is disturbed. You represent her mother and it distresses her that you will leave. Her sense of abandonment will affect her all her life.

'Miss Reinhart I am so sorry, it is my fault entirely, I should have been more sensitive to the situation. I did not think this would occur. I understand if you do not wish to return here again.'

We reached the entrance where I retrieved my hat and coat from its peg with a trembling hand and turned to face her.

'Miss De Bours, twenty four years ago my twin sister lived and died here. I wish to know what became of her. I wish to know what sort of a life she led whether it was a life of misfortune or otherwise, therefore, based upon that fact, and even when it pains me to do so, I will return.'

Two

Institution for Foundlings and Orphans, Greenwich - 1881

Leah

She was seated by the window with her gaze fixed ahead in steady concentration, but it was actually the fly I spotted first. Her eyes were glued to it as it crawled up and down, smacking its furry body against the glass. I noticed that her attention never wavered, not even for a second, as if she was engaged in some study of a scientific nature.

The older staff at the orphanage had informed me that she was five years of age, mute, and prone to aggressive outbursts, but I found the information almost impossible to believe as I witnessed the way her soft hair curled at the very tips, and her tiny lips formed a delicate pout.

Her name was Primrose, but it was Pixie they called her. It seemed to matter very little however, as she did not respond to her name. Not even when I walked up closely to her and mouthed *Pixie* to her face. There was nothing in her clear blue eyes that told me she was interested in my presence, let alone that she might recognise or respond to a simple word. She wore a serious expression which was transfixed upon the insect as though it was the only living thing within her realm of existence.

What this child must have endured I could not possibly imagine though she had a good padding of flesh upon her, so I surmised that she had come from a comfortable home where food, if not plentiful, would have been steadily supplied. She was pretty in a tomboyish sort of way, and if one was to capture a simple image of her, they might say she was just a commonplace infant with no peculiarity of any sort.

I whispered to her gently. 'My name is Leah.'

Silence.

'She won't answer you.'

I jumped at the voice behind me.

It was Sister Ernestine. She was standing with a towel folded in her arms and a large bar of soap placed on top. I noticed that rarely did the nurse move about empty-handed. Her starched apron revealed deep creases due to the way it stretched across her robust bosom and her thick ankles spilled over her practical footwear.

Despite her noticeably large frame the middle-aged woman appeared to be able to dash about attending to her duties with great ease. We both stood for a moment watching the new girl as her eyes followed the moving insect.

'Will she not respond to anyone at all?' I enquired.

Sister shrugged. 'It seems not. The poor little nipper had a nasty fall apparently. Knocked her head and damaged her spine. She can hear, but she won't talk. Who knows what's in her head. They say it's a permanent thing though Miss Leah, so don't waste all your efforts. Don't forget to fetch the linen for the babies bath-time won't you.'

'Yes Sister,' I replied.

It was Sister's way of telling me to move on and not stall my duties to dally about with this new admission, but I wondered if with a bit of time and patience the girl could be reached. She seemed curious enough.

Even though I had only been employed at the orphanage a few months, I had come to grow fond of the orphans there. I felt that I understood them. My obvious affection for them, however, was frowned upon by my new employers, but it was my nature to be affectionate even though I was only fourteen years of age and not much more than a child myself.

I quickly learned that the orphanage cared for children of all ages but did not like to accept those above the age of twelve. It was thought that after that age they could find employment of their own, or enter a workhouse even though many were full to the brim.

On my arrival I noticed that many had an unusual disability or ailment, a troublesome twitch, a strange gait, or perhaps some were just slow to understand instructions of any sort. Others refused to speak, or they looked away vacantly each time you came close. There was no doubt that some of the orphans would certainly be classified as a little 'peculiar.'

There seemed to be fewer older children in the orphanage too, for if they did not arrive in a sorrowful condition, it was feared they might sooner or later perish from having lived such a tough life on the streets.

Some simply vanished now and again, often without trace through the thick tangle of trees and bushes which surrounded the building. I had wept only six days past when one young lad escaped early one morning to embark on an unwitting sense of freedom, only to be killed by a horse rearing a corner too fast on some narrow lane.

With these sort of things occurring now and then I found it persistently worrying that I would grow too much affection for the orphans. To have a child perish in front of your eyes, or disappear into the cold harsh landscape was an experience I did not wish to repeat.

I viewed Pixie's face which was still fixed on the window or the scene beyond. She had shown no desire to acknowledge me. I watched her quietly and sensed a pure innocence within her.

'Miss Leah are you still wasting time with that girl?' Sister barked again from behind. 'Please hurry and get to work helping me bath the babies.'

I promptly left Pixie then and walked over to the large cupboard to collect a pile of linen, napkins and safety pins then hurried across to the adjacent room where a large steel tub of warm water was placed near the hearth.

My duties were varied and often more akin to a housemaid than an orphanage carer, for they included scrubbing soiled napkins, plus other frightful necessities, such as helping Sister wash the fragile babies once a fortnight and hoping none would drown. The wriggling babies were all now laid out on towels on the floor ready for a refreshing wash.

'There we are. I wash, you can dry,' Sister said as she lifted the infant closest to her and removed the fabric he was swaddled in. He still hadn't quite woken up and gave a little yawn.

She held the infant in a good grip and quickly dipped him into the soapy water cupping her hand to collect water and splashing it over his head. His tiny waxy hands outstretched instantly and he began to wail in response, his little arms and legs flailing wildly.

I took hold of him taking great care not to let his slippery body fall from my grasp and keep his tiny head from sinking beneath the water. I managed to lift him out and towel him dry, tie a piece of square linen between his legs with a safety pin and swaddle him in a blanket, before settling him back in a large basket where all the infants would sleep together.

After all the babies were bathed I piled up the soiled laundry and took it to the boiler room.

When I returned Sister had already taken the babies to their quarters so I returned next door to check on Pixie. No-one had attended to her because it appeared that she did not make a sound or call attention to herself.

'Hello Pixie,' I said a little nervously.

She was sitting in the same position I had left her. In a high backed wooden chair with two rickety wheels at the bottom of it so that it could be tipped back and pushed along like an odd sort of upright wheelbarrow.

'Do you need anything?' I asked. She began to rock back and forth clutching a cloth doll to her chest, making a smacking sound as her back hit the chair.

I picked up a cup from a tray and placed it to her lips and she stopped still for a moment to sip noisily, water spilling down the corners of her mouth.

Despite Sister's earlier warning I sat with her for some minutes, careful not to sit too closely however, for it seemed that her manner of rocking seemed to intensify when I did so.

Instead I introduced myself, telling her of my upbringing and how I came to be working at the orphanage. It was as sad a story to tell as any I might think up in my fertile imagination, but I was certain that Pixie, (if she would talk,) would sympathise with me, or perhaps one day she might place her tender cheek upon my lap so that I might stroke her hair.

I went on to explain that all the occurrences within the orphanage walls were never to be spoken of externally, (not that she would speak to any persons about any particular thing, of course,) but I informed her anyway. Quite why I felt it necessary to tell her of the orphanage's rules I did not know, though she did appear to calm at the lull of my voice and I hoped that it might establish a trusting bond between us.

When I had first arrived I was taught to answer the children's persistent questions as to why they were brought here. Each day I was expected to remind the older ones that they were most fortunate, because Mrs Featherstone who ran the orphanage, often reiterated that many children were left daily on the streets to die, discarded as little more than products of waste.

'You will be cared for here,' I told her. 'Any child brought to this godly haven will find it a better place to exist than to perish in a gutter upon some filthy concrete pavement.'

She cocked her head sideways at those words, and for a moment I thought she had understood. I did not feel it appropriate to tell her that there appeared to be many rooms in the orphanage in which I was forbidden to enter. Or that Miss Jeannie, my room companion, said it was because there were dead bodies inside them, and that hideous experiments were conducted on the bodies.

I soon learned that Miss Jeannie was very good at sarcastic and far-fetched remarks, so I never paid her words much attention, but I could admit to feeling very uncomfortable walking past some of those locked doors.

I ploughed on with my explanations, but I could not tell how much she digested, for she sat staring at the hills in the distance which were now beginning to disappear behind a blanket of grey mist.

My communications to her were suddenly interrupted when I saw her small mouth move into a little O shape. Then a high pitched squeal emanated from her lips. I wondered if she had become excited at the appearance of a small bird that descended upon the window sill.

Was she trying to capture its attention?

She lifted a little finger and tapped at the glass. My eyes widened with excitement. She was trying to communicate with the bird. I leaned toward her and took her delicate hand away from the window and into my own so that she would face me.

'Yes it is a baby bird. Perhaps it's mother has built a small nest above the window.' I mouthed the word... *bird...* but her delighted expression dropped and seemed to turn into one of terror.

'It is all right,' I said in an attempt to reassure her. But quite out of turn she recoiled, placing her hands over her ears before emitting a loud scream. The sound pierced the air so loudly that Sister Ernestine must have been alerted nearby for she came charging in with an exasperated expression.

'Get away from her. She might bite you.'

I stood to my feet, shocked that she might react in such a way. There was no sense to this sudden commotion for she had been so relaxed just a few seconds before.

'Right, you bad child,' Sister Ernestine said as she took hold of the chair and began to wheel the screaming girl out of the room.

I had expected Pixie would sleep with other girls of her age but Sister Ernestine took a sharp turn in the opposite direction and headed down the candle-lit corridor to a room at the far end of the building. One which I was certain had been off limits.

'Where are you taking her?' I asked.

'To her own room. You can't expect her to stay with the others.'

I stared at her in confusion and she frowned. 'Just help me get her inside.'

I followed as she took a large bunch of keys from her pocket and opened the door to reveal a sparsely furnished room which accommodated a cot bed with a mattress, and in the far corner there sat a dresser beneath the window where a pitiful excuse for a curtain hung limply over the glass.

'Help me get her onto the bed,' she instructed.

I watched as Pixie wriggled in an effort to free herself from Sister's grip.

'Oh you wretched little thing,' Sister spat.

Pixie's face became inflamed with an effort to escape the tightened grip and I watched in shock, having never witnessed such a commotion before.

'Miss Cunningham. Will you please assist me?' Sister barked, and I was jolted into action. Between us we managed to pin her down on to the bed, and there I was to witness an event which would not escape my mind for some time to come.

Sister brought out a small glass bottle and a spoon from her apron. 'Now you hold her whilst I get this down her.' I held her still as the tonic was forced into her mouth. The girl swallowed the fluid and sobbed until finally she became limp.

'She's all spent,' Sister pronounced. From under the bed she produced two large straps which she buckled crossways over her torso and legs, securing them with clasps to either side of the bed. The child lay panting, her tiny chest rising and falling.

‘She'll sleep the night through. Let's leave her to it.’

I looked at the helpless girl and felt tears fill my eyes.

‘But she is so young,’ I said.

Sister glared at me.

‘We ain't got time here to give them all fancy treatment Miss Cunningham. There's a hundred others in this orphanage needing us, and this little demon will turn all the others wild if we let her. Now get back to your duties and think no more of it. No harm will come to her.’

I walked to the door and looked back, committing the image of the restrained child into my memory. I paused to think if I had ever witnessed such a sorrowful sight in my entire life, and realised that I had most certainly not. The young girl turned her head and her eyes followed me to the door.

Sister closed the door behind us, bolting it shut and everything became silent. I walked back along the hallway knowing that my life would not be the same again. Not now that this damaged and fragile child had so unexpectedly come into my world.

Three

Leah

I did not see Pixie again for several days. Sister Ernestine forbid me to enter her room. I was uncertain whether she arranged this to prevent me from providing the girl with any sort of comfort, or so that I would not witness the impromptu fits from which she appeared to suffer.

My desire was to check on her, if only to reassure myself that she was not in distress, but each time I found the courage to enquire upon her welfare I was met with a stern glare and orders to keep away.

'She needs breaking in so she does,' Mrs O'Flaherty, exclaimed when I questioned her in the dining hall. I also asked her whether Pixie would ever be able to consume her meals with the rest of the children.

'The girl is un-tamed and completely unpredictable,' she replied. 'She'll end all her antics if she knows what's good for her.'

I felt her words to be overly harsh, but I had expected no less. Mrs O'Flaherty was not the sort of woman to adopt a softened approach. Her words were often cutting and her manner severe. She also appeared to be a great believer in locking up the children alone. It was not unusual to see her dragging a child by one arm across the floor in order to ensconce them within a room or cupboard.

'Let that be a lesson to the rest of you. Children must reflect upon their actions,' I would hear her say to a group of small timid faces.

There had been a few occasions when Mrs O'Flaherty forgot about a child she had incarcerated, and one could hear the bangs and feeble cries of distress continuing into the early hours of the morning. Eventually a person would hear the cries and rescue the poor child.

Normally the lists of tasks I was made to perform came from Sister Ernestine or Mrs Featherstone, the lady in charge of the day to day running of the orphanage, who had a very strange way of being utterly pleasing one moment, and stern the next.

It wasn't unusual that I might be instructed to perform a set of tasks for the morning, then Miss Jeannie would arrive with renewed instructions from Sister to discontinue and perform another.

That is exactly what occurred several days after Miss Pixie's incarceration when I was cleaning the floor in my own quarters and Miss Jeannie walked into the room.

'You are to attend to the girl in the chair,' she said with a serious look on her face.

'Whatever do you mean?' I stood to my feet and she rolled her eyes as though I was utterly ignorant.

'You know. The peculiar girl who arrived last week. Mrs Featherstone sent me and told me to tell you to fetch her from her room and take her out into the fresh air for exactly one hour and no longer.'

She held out a key and I took it from her.

How was I to be made entirely responsible for a girl suffering severe difficulties, I pondered. There had to be some mistake. Surely she required adult assistance.

'Are you to accompany me?' I asked Jeannie, suddenly fearful of the prospect as my mind recalled the girl's harrowing screams.

'No. I am required to take care of other matters today,' she said and promptly flounced away.

I stared at the key in my hand willing my heart to stop beating so loudly, then dusting my apron I left the room and walked the entire length of the hallway to the room Sister Ernestine had led me to a week earlier. I could not understand the necessity to keep the door locked since the poor child could obviously not escape. Nonetheless, I felt my hand tremble as I turned the key inside the lock where no sound could be heard as I slowly opened the door.

She lay on her side, one small hand clutching a corner of the blanket which she pressed gently to one cheek.

She was facing the wall so she did not see me approach the bed where sturdy metal rails had been positioned to prevent her from falling to the floor.

I stood as closely as I dared.

'Good morning Miss Pixie,' I said.

She did not respond.

I stepped a little closer and she turned her head to look at me. Perhaps it was a foolish thing but I tried to act as though I was an extremely relaxed individual in her presence, but when I spoke I could still detect a tremor in my voice.

'It is a lovely morning, Miss Pixie. I think we could take a little stroll through the grounds, what do you think?'

Her eyes flicked over to me and I took hold of the handles on her wooden chair and wheeled it closer to the bed, motioning that I would like to seat her inside it. Then I was surprised by her arms coming up towards me, a sign that she was content for me to do so. I gently lifted her, noticing how light her body felt in my arms.

'I will strap you to your chair then we will not waste another moment inside this room.'

She remained calm which did not illicit any great surprise, since the child had probably not left the room since first being locked inside it. Though she somehow seemed a different child to the one which I had first encountered. Perhaps the last day or two had calmed her and Mrs O'Flaherty was correct, for who was I to make any sense of her condition or judge the treatment afforded to her?

Strapping her securely with the belt I noticed that her hair seemed to have caught in a tangle. I made a mental note to comb through it later and then passed her the cloth doll, which she clutched tightly to her chest. Lastly, I wrapped a thick shawl across her shoulders then together we left the room.

A few orphans passing in the hallway threw us curious stares but I made my way to the exit door at the exterior of the building to avoid encountering too many persons.

Pixie sat silently as I pushed her chair along the path towards the back of the orphanage where she could see the village clock-tower between tall rows of trees. She stared open-mouthed at the view showing a twinkle of delight in her eyes. Occasionally she would glance back as if to check that I was still behind her.

I pointed out the small chapel as we passed it, and the old mill in the hills beyond, but I had no idea whether she had been accustomed to life in a city or a more rural setting. I slowed down to show her a clump of pale yellow bulbs which had recently sprung from the bottom of a thick row of hedges which divided the orphanage from vacant miles of farmland.

'These will be daffodils soon, they will be as bright and pretty as the sun.'

She focused on the buds, gently placing a fingertip on one.

'Yes, daffodils Pixie, and do you know that such pretty flowers have leaves too?' I plucked a leaf from its stem and gently handed it to her, but she shrank away.

'It is just a harmless little leaf.' I laughed and allowed it to fall to the ground. A flock of crows flew overhead and she looked upwards in fear.

'Oh those are such noisy birds, they have frightful black eyes, but they won't hurt you.' Her eyes followed them across the sky.

Finally we stopped and I sat upon a stone seat positioning her chair to face the hills beyond. A tiny goldfinch perched its feet at the edge of the gentle stream which wound its way around the orphanage.

'I used to live a little distance away from here,' I said, pointing at the general direction of the village.

'At least I did so when my mother was alive and my father cared for me.'

I checked her face for a response but there was none.

'My mother passed away just one year ago, and my father suffered a great deal of grief. After that I only seemed to get in the way of him, and so I was made to come here.'

She continued to stare vacantly ahead. Despite the lack of acknowledgement it was a relief to be able to talk openly to a person without judgement or recrimination.

'I will tell you about my life Pixie, but I do not wish to burden you with my sorrow. If only you could in turn tell me how you feel I might be able to assist you better. In any case, I'm certain that you would like to come here again, wouldn't you?'

She tilted her head forward resting her eyes on some curiously shaped stones on the ground.

'Have you ever played on the grass, Pixie? Have you ever felt a stone inside your hand?'

I picked up the smallest stone I could find and placed it on her lap. She touched it with one finger then enclosed it within a small fist, opening and closing her fingers slowly to feel its weight and texture within her palm. She then reached out and offered the stone back to me. I took it from her and laughed loudly then handed it back, and this we did for many moments, an activity she appeared to enjoy, until the temperature dipped a few degrees and we set off back towards the main building with her cheeks having produced a rosy bloom.

We entered through the back door where I could push her chair up a set of wider steps in order to reach her room, though I perspired at the effort and half way up Sister Ernestine appeared looking agitated.

'Where are you going with this girl?'

I swallowed nervously. 'I was instructed by Mrs Featherstone to take her for a stroll,' I replied with honesty.

She spat back, 'For a stroll? Are we now to treat the orphans as guests in some fancy accommodation?'

She shook her head disapprovingly.

'This girl will be spoiled and encouraged to be awkward with that kind of activity. Off you go and take her back to her room, leave the key in the office as I'll be taking up her meal shortly.'

I continued up the stairs without any assistance from Sister and once inside the room I wheeled her chair to the window and saw that the stone sat on her lap. I leaned closely to her ear, pleased that she was so much better behaved than during our first encounter.

'You can keep the stone, but we mustn't let Sister see it. I will put it in your locker,' I told her.

No doubt the woman would disapprove and likely inform Mrs Featherstone of my carelessness.

'And pay little attention to what Sister Ernestine says about me. If I can I will be the one to come back for you soon.'

I turned to leave as her eyes once again rested on the window and I saw that the glow in her cheeks had already begun to fade.

Before I could stop myself I locked the door and departed, wondering how she could have been abandoned because of her ailment, for she had shown herself to be sensitive and communicative, unlike the portrayal of her character given by others.

After that morning she had placed herself a little deeper into my heart and I found that I could think of little else for the rest of that day as I continued with my duties.

Four

Leah

Mrs Featherstone handed me a blank diary that she explained had been kept inside her cupboard because she had never found the time to fill it in with any sort of interesting detail.

I was thrilled with the unexpected gift.

I had merely approached her with the hope of obtaining some sort of writing utensil, explaining that I would like to practice some of my skills once I had retired to my quarters late at night.

In reality my intention was to log Pixie's activities but rather than berate me for such an imprudent question, Mrs Featherstone appeared impressed to learn that I had even acquired such a valuable skill as writing.

A diary was a fancy item I had never owned before, not even prior to my mother's death. When we lived in relative comfort I rarely received any such valuable gift. My short-lived run of educational instruction was achieved by her insistence, for as far as my father was concerned, girls did not require nor benefit from the purpose of an education.

It was thanks to Aunt Mabel, my now deceased aunt, that I even obtained such an opportunity. She often wrote lengthy letters to my mother to inform her of the great opportunities young girls were procuring as governesses in the coastal town of Scarborough.

She emphasised that even if my father rejected the idea, times were changing for young women. Many were becoming skilled in administrative procedures and my mother ought to do all she could to ensure that I received at least some preliminary tuition in learning the alphabet, along with the usual guidance in cookery and domestic house-keeping skills.

Quite unexpectedly one day, Aunt Mabel forwarded her sister a small sum of money. It was tucked within an envelope which my mother promptly put towards enrolment, securing a classroom seat at a nearby school for young ladies.

There I spent three short months learning to read and write before I was made to return home because mother tragically passed away.

Devastated with grief, my father lost his position and frittered away the remaining money on ale and gambling activities. I could do nothing but sit and watch as my own father preferred to drown in his sorrows rather than see his daughter take further steps towards a more promising future.

A few weeks after my mother's death I turned fourteen years of age and my father succumbed almost completely to the habit of drink, his misery being only partially alleviated by a newly developed passion for the serving lady at the drinking establishment he frequented.

Four weeks later I was wrenched from the familiarity of my home and brought to the orphanage on account of the workhouses being too full. My position was to assist the staff here and I was pleased that my new-found skills accompanied me, even though I did not know if they would be of any use.

Sitting alone in my bedroom now and watching the sun hazily descend behind the hills, I decided to open up and record my very first entry.

Miss Pixie (or Primrose)

Pixie is five years of age, her eyes are a soft blue and I think she is very fair of face. Today she took a great degree of interest in an unremarkable looking stone which she held in her hand then passed back to me. I hope that she learns a lot more in the future and if she is slow to learn, I will be more than content to teach her.

I closed the diary, my wrist already tiring of balancing the pen, the use of which I was little accustomed to.

Just as I carefully slid the diary beneath the mattress the door opened, and in strode Miss Jeannie with two coiled springs of hair set loose on either side of her face. She wore a solemn expression.

'Have I ever told you how much I despise this place?' she complained, slumping onto her bed to untie her boots.

'Yes you have,' I replied. 'You have told me quite often as a matter of fact, who has upset you?'

Miss Jeannie was easily disgruntled by even the smallest of occurrences.

'Mrs O'Flaherty in the dining hall. If she wasn't such an ogre and bellowed all the time, my ears might not be so horrifically inflated.'

I smiled at her exaggeration. Miss Jeannie rarely had a good word to say regarding the orphanage staff, this being in complete contrast to the young men she encountered at the Saturday evening dances she attended in the village hall.

There was a Patrick and a James, or was it Jack? It mattered not, for Miss Jeannie could not decide which boy she held the most affection for, and each Sunday evening I was required to hear the events until I drifted off to the sound of her high-pitched excitement.

She quickly removed her outer garments and donned her sleeping gown before finally settling beneath the blanket and tucking it up to her chin.

'I do wish I could make something more of my life, Miss Leah. Oh, and what is it you were hiding away when I walked in? It looked very secretive.'

'It is nothing,' I said defensively.

She sat upright and stared at me suspiciously.

'You are a dark horse Miss Leah. I am certain there is more to you than you let on. Have you something illicit beneath your bed?'

My cheeks blazed with guilt. She would find the diary anyway and there would be no secrets kept. I stubbornly refused to hand it over until she leapt out of her bed to wrestle with me and managed to wrench it from my grasp.

'You may look, but it is not to be read by any other person!' I said sharply.

I was glad that I had not yet begun to fill it with too many details.

'Oh my, such a pretty diary. I did not know that you could write. You are so very fortunate.'

She traced a fingertip across the delicately embroidered cover designed in the shape of dandelions and acorns, then forgetting her manners she began to leaf through the pages.

'Are you able to read?' I asked her.

'Yes, a little.' She rolled her eyes. 'Actually no, not very well at all. Will you read it to me?'

She passed it back to me and returned to her bed.

I read out the short phrase I had written, glancing across to gauge her interest, but she only squinted upwards at the ceiling.

'Why do you care what this one orphan girl does or feels?' she asked. 'Is it not the case that every orphan here needs an equal amount of care?'

'Yes, I know that they do,' I replied. 'I just don't know why Pixie must be locked away in a room all on her own.'

She glanced across at me, twisting a ringlet around one finger.

'Well from what I have come to learn, it is because she is possessed.'

'Possessed?' I repeated, my eyes widening.

'Yes. Peculiar of mind. Apparently she took a bite out of Mrs Featherstone's arm when she first arrived. Poor Mrs Featherstone had to be attended to by Sister Ernestine and there was a terrible commotion downstairs. The girl seemed beside herself with fury.'

'Did something occur which caused her to act in such a way?' I pressed further.

'Not here,' she said emphatically. 'We have been told that the girl had suffered an accident which seems to have turned her into a wilful beast. I think you should not pay too much attention to her Miss Leah. It is best not to invest too much of yourself, as Mrs Featherstone keeps reminding us, for if we create too many feelings they will only serve to cloud our good judgement.

Feelings cloud judgement.

I felt an urge to write the words in the diary for some reason, but refrained.

'It may well end up that she could be sent to the asylum on Barnett Street. I heard some of the staff whisper it. You know, the place where they chain you to the wall. They say that the evil ghosts whisper at you there day and night, causing an even worse kind of madness than the one you were admitted there with in the first place!'

I covered my mouth with my hand. 'No, stop! That is awful. Pixie showed very little signs of disobedience in my presence. I found her quite calm, and she communicates with me.'

Jeannie's eyebrows shot up.

'She spoke to you?'

'No, not with words, but in her expressions and actions. She spoke very clearly with her actions.'

'Well we shall see, won't we?' she said, turning to face the wall.

'I must sleep now Miss Leah, please snuff out the candle and remember, we will be taking the children to Mass in the morning and I do not wish to be yawning the entire time again. I am sure my lungs have still not recovered from the punishment of being made to re-fill the coal scuttle to the brim for an entire week.'

I pushed the diary back into the crevice between the mattress and bed frame and snuffed out the candle, wondering if Pixie would be allowed to attend the service, or that I might be permitted to take her for a stroll again. If I spoke to Mrs Featherstone about her good behaviour and how she had interacted with me, she might then see that the girl held some promise with regard to her character, that all she really required was a little patience and understanding.

In the dormitory below my bed I could hear the silent sniffles and cries of children who missed their parents, the sad lamentations that they might once have had the delight of knowing them. I longed to comfort them, but I was forbidden to attend to the orphans after sundown. Nor was I allowed to embrace them or offer much physical contact, for we were told they would become insolently spoiled and *molly-coddling* would only hinder them from acquiring a necessary independence.

It would be frightfully lonely for Pixie in her room. I wondered whether her eyes were now closed. Was she in a deep contented slumber? Or were her tears dampening her pillow as she pressed the corner of the blanket to her cheek. I felt a pressing urge to go to her, to pick her up in my arms like a fragile porcelain doll and hold her in an attempt to make her whole again, the natural instinct coming upon me like an unexpected wave crashing over a rock.

I decided that I would try to get to the matter of her heart and mind and also do my best to keep a record of the results of her actions.

Everything had fallen into a restful silence.

I closed my eyes and allowed my thoughts to loosen their tight grip. It was for a very short time however, as the chatter of children in the hallways attending the breakfast hall woke me sharply and I was to rise and begin my duties all over again.

——[——

The old chapel was situated in an extended part of the building close to a thick iron gate at the west of the orphanage. It stood beneath a towering and impressive leafy elm tree, and no matter whether it was viewed near or far, nothing betrayed it as a house of God other than a splintered wooden crucifix that had been nailed to the top of a wooden door.

The children stood stiff and uncomfortable inside the cramped confinement. Several rows of sleepy faces, tousled hair, and poorly constructed

Sunday shoes made of discarded rags stared blankly at the altar, as Father Menza lifted the cup to his thin lips which contained the sacred blood of Jesus Christ.

For the children it was a typical Sunday morning routine, nothing more was to be expected other than that they must behave in a godly fashion and as a reward for this act of obedience they would receive the body of Christ into their hungry little mouths.

Father said that to receive the Eucharist was a privilege, and by far more sustaining than a mere crumb or two of bread. I could not help but wonder if Father himself had ever felt the painful stab of hunger inside his belly. I watched as the pitiful little faces with lowered eyes chewed on the thin wafer silently.

From where I stood I was mostly out of view, and having looked around I saw no sign of Pixie at all. Had she been forgotten? I fidgeted nervously from leg to leg. Surely her disability should not prevent her from entering the house of our Lord? My eyes scanned the room for Sister Ernestine. I caught sight of her a few feet away pulling apart two young boys who had got into a scuffle. I made a mental note to approach her after the service to make an enquiry. With this in mind the morning's sermon seemed to go on forever with Father Menza speaking in a voice so audibly low that even those positioned at the front of the chapel must have strained their ears to hear him.

Such was the lack of air in that confined space that I was glad to hear the bell ring and be let outside. We led the children past the exterior of the building up a small hill, and back inside the orphanage where I managed to catch Sister's attention as she walked briskly ahead.

'How is Miss Pixie today?' I asked.

She rolled her eyes. 'Well she didn't seem too content this morning. I thought it best not to bring her along. She's due her luncheon now anyway. Why do you ask, Miss Leah?'

'May I take her meal up to her?' I replied hopefully.

She cast a suspicious eye at me.

'Oh go on then, you might have better luck with her than I do, the nasty little nipper spat all her egg on my lap this morning.'

I stifled a giggle. I could imagine why Pixie would do such a thing. The boiled eggs were always stone cold by the time they were dished out from the kitchen.

Sister handed me a key from her pocket.

'If you like her so much why don't you take charge of her for a couple of days? Maybe you have a better knack with her. She'll need assistance with feeds and washes and if you're not careful she might bite you now and again. Do you still want to take her on board?'

I nodded without hesitation. 'Yes I do.'

'I'll check with Mrs Featherstone then, but I am sure it will be fine for now, let's see how you get on with her,' she added, seemingly pleased to be rid of the girl, though I hurried away quickly before she came up with a reason to change her mind.

After retrieving a light snack of broth and bread, I made my way to her room. I unlocked the door quietly so as not to startle her and found her propped up against a pillow focusing on the doll in her hand.

'Good morning Pixie, do you remember me? I have brought you something to eat.'

She did not look at me nor did her expression change. I decided that if she was being purposely ignorant then I was going to have to try much harder to win her trust all over again. I set the tray down on the table beside her bed and pulled a chair close to her. I smiled, hiding my nerves as best I could manage, noticing her dull complexion.

'Let me help you take a few spoonfuls of broth but if you do not want it, do not struggle with me. I have no desire to force feed you or make you do anything against your will. Though I will say that refusing your food means that you could very well become poorly, and if that was to occur you would have to remain in bed, and then we cannot take any more refreshing walks outside can we?'

Her eyes met mine for a second, where I thought something in my voice seemed to register. I brought the bowl closer to her chin and lifted a spoonful of fluid to her mouth. She sipped at its edge. My heart inflated with joy.

'Just a few more of these spoons now Miss Pixie, and we can then take another walk, which I know you so like.'

She responded positively, and if I had not known her well enough I would have sworn she gave me a little smile. I wiped her chin then set down the bowl.

'Now I shall just check with Mrs Featherstone regarding our walk and then we shall...'

At that moment the door burst open and Miss Jeannie walked in.

'Oh Miss Leah, you must come downstairs immediately.'

'Whatever is wrong?' I asked.

'Mrs Featherstone is inside her office quarrelling with a gentleman very loudly. In fact it was so loud that I heard every word from the hallway as I happened to be passing by her office on my duties.'

I bit my lip. 'But what does this have to do with me?'

She lowered her voice to a whisper.

'I think the gentleman in question may be your father.'

Five

Annie

I reclined in my favourite chair with the folder containing the details and notes regarding my sister placed on my lap.

On a typical weekday afternoon I would normally be pre-occupied with sorting and assembling the paint brushes and pots scattered across the table following a class with one of my students, but the singular session scheduled for today had ended earlier than I expected.

Miss Wilding had complained of a headache, and being unable to concentrate on the lesson she returned home to ease her discomfort.

Knowing that I could at last browse through the paperwork I had brought home from the orphanage warmed my heart greatly, though it also set upon me an edge of nervousness that I could not easily describe. That I might now twenty-four years after the tragic event itself find out what had become of Pixie seemed inconceivable, just as her life and death seemed at times to be almost fictitious.

I had been inside my bedroom at the time of the accident. My only recollection of the event was that I had left her alone in the garden, but having no accurate estimation of the passing of time at such a tender age, I can only assume we played together for a short period of time. A commotion seemed to ensue downstairs some time later and I was not permitted to leave my bedroom.

After that I never saw Pixie again. She became a ghost in my mind and it was there she seemed to have frozen, like some faded old portrait outlined in a buttery glow, immortalised with her hair set into the same manner of two glossy coils of yellow extended from either side of her head.

I remembered how as a child it was like staring into a mirror each time I faced her. I had, in an innocent way, adored her. Perhaps not as a parent might adore a child, but in the way a young girl might feel affection for a doll which she carries tightly to her chest.

If I were to unfold my memories like a long scroll, that fateful day would be etched there like some dark stain. Her disappearance cast a shadow on my heart. I became the owner of a childlike grief that I could never quite make sense of, heal from, or encounter some form of release.

My parents seemed stricken into silence in the aftermath of the accident, but strangely, they remained resolutely silent on the matter. We each of us caused the steady vibrations in the house to shift from light and airy to dark and sombre. A large canvas sat fading in the corner of the room gathering dust because Mother promptly stopped painting and never resumed again. Father's beloved chess set languished in the opposite corner of the room with its pieces still awaiting the resumption of a half played game.

Time stood imperfectly still.

And everything, including ourselves, moved forward with great difficulty.

'Mama! Where is Pixie?'

I remember crying at the hem of her skirt as she sat one evening at her dresser, wearily reaching for the pins to set free her long golden hair, allowing it to cascade over her shoulders.

'She is gone Annie, it is better to forget her.'

'Gone where?'

'Just gone. Now be a good girl and go to bed.'

These words, so many years later, still resonate in my head. We seemed to exist from then on inside a slow-moving translucency of greyish tones, caught inside some deadened and silent atmosphere.

Our servants were lined up and ordered to refrain from passing comment, or proffering questions. They were hardly permitted to speak at all, and that which they must speak of would be relevant to their duties alone, nothing more.

I watched Mother travel throughout the day from room to room as though a hefty weight accompanied her. Her delicate hand often rose from her lap to her temple, and at intervals, I would notice the lines crease on her forehead as though she had just again been informed of the same frightful news.

I was shocked to witness, just a week after Pixie left, my mother drawing back the curtains to let in the sun's warm rays of light. She also changed her black mourning gown to a darker shade of blue, then promptly resumed her daily affairs with her usual stilted decorum.

It was as though suddenly, she had decided that my sister was no longer worth remembering, that her life had come and gone and we were to act as though she had never been a part of us at all.

Father admonished me one day in the dining room when I refused to eat my supper without Pixie's chair, plate and cup placed beside my own. I could not understand why all trace of her ought to be erased.

Pixie was not gone, not in my heart nor in my mind, which seemed to my parents to be something of an irritant. That I still loved and yearned for my twin to return did little more than cause them anxiety and an even more fervent desire to erase her from my memory. I could only conclude that she had indeed suffered a grave accident, and for reasons unknown, my parents had decided to give her up as one might discard a broken porcelain doll.

I stared at the folder and shivered with anticipation, my thoughts having provoked a fear in digesting its contents.

What might I find within these pages that might prove distressing?

The only information provided to me about her life and death was accidentally unearthed the day after my twentieth birthday celebrations.

Fuelled by annoyance over a parade of suitors during the party, suitors which I had stubbornly rejected, I openly resented Mother's view that I would soon be left *on the shelf*.

Descending into a sulk following the quarrel we had engaged in, I disappeared for a few hours into Father's study. It was there that I came across some information lying on his desk. I presumed that he had forgotten to file away the paperwork, but nevertheless, the discovery shocked me to the very core.

The records were dated fifteen years prior and were 'scant' to say the least. Just a single record of information.

It stated that Pixie had been relocated to a suitable establishment where the care offered to her would outweigh the *quality of care* within the original family home.

I could not make sense of it.

How could any other location be better for Pixie than remaining with her own flesh and blood?

> A transfer to the orphanage for the infant is the most logical way to proceed - following a great trauma to the body resulting in paralysis of the limb.

The record showed that Pixie had been sent to the Greenwich Orphanage, and checking the dates of her admittance there, they seemed to comply with her disappearance. Up until that point my parents had refused to tell me where she had been taken, only that she was damaged beyond repair after a fall and would not be able to lead a normal existence.

Beneath that inscription I read an entry of death which simply said.

Infant - orphan female.

A record of the deceased is hereby entered on 14th October 1882

Cause of death - choking

Pixie was just six years old at the time of her death, but there was nothing substantial, scientifically otherwise, that would reveal the important details of her preliminary injury which had so cruelly marked her destiny.

How did the accident occur?

How did her death occur?

I brought the information to both my parents who stared at each other in silence. It was, and had always been, a subject too gigantic to discuss and their silence did nothing to help heal our already fractured relationship.

My own happiness declined further as Mother persisted on having me wed any suitable bachelor, (preferably one in possession of a great deal of money.) Father was less persistent and encouraged my great enthusiasm of art and my desire to study in depth, for I had inherited the ability from my mother who, prior to Pixie's injury, painted only as a creative pursuit.

I however, did not wish my abilities to go to waste.

The subject of Pixie was once again laid to rest that day, but as the years slowly passed a great chasm of resentment filled me. When Father passed away a few years ago my inheritance entitlement came into maturity. I promptly moved into my current modest residence taking our housekeeper Mrs Byrne with me, for I knew my mother disliked the timid woman but had never had the bad grace to leave her without employment.

It was a scandalous move on my part, though Mother had agreed that we would fare better under a separate roof. When I headed for the door with a case full of belongings she begged me not to cast myself into the role of spinsterhood for the rest of my life.

I had no deliberate plan to do as she feared, but I could match her persistence with my own stubbornness. I cared little about her concerns or how she fretted over the opinions of those in the upper echelons of our society.

All I desired was to live a fulfilling life, a life that Pixie could *not* live. When I felt I truly wished to marry, it would be based on love and not dependency.

It seemed to me, however, that even when I had managed to extricate myself from her manipulations and cloying needs, I would still be affected by her own private sufferings.

Not long after my departure from home Mother suffered a nervous breakdown and was admitted into a care home facility. She refused to return home, stating that she could no longer bear to live alone without my father.

Perhaps it was I who had caused her to gradually lose her mind with my stubborn desire for complete independence as well as our differences over the years.

I could not say for certain. I just knew that my relationship with Mother had always been one of a complex and difficult nature.

Inhaling deeply now I opened the folder only to find myself becoming instantly disappointed. It contained only a few pieces of paper with some formal entries and various handwritten notes that seemed to be haphazardly thrown together in a badly organised pile.

I closely observed the first piece of paper. It was a couple of stamped and verified circus tickets. There was also a piece of paper with a handwritten list addressed to Leah, a list of items and linens she was to collect from the basement.

There was nothing else written there so I cast it to one side. I picked up a pen and made a note to enquire upon a female named Leah when I next visited the orphanage. I had promised Miss De Bours that I would return once I had digested the correspondence and furthermore, I would pose any questions which I had.

I consulted the clock and saw that it was already after midnight. Bertie appeared from nowhere and entwined his sleek tawny body between my legs, meowing loudly to remind me that I had completely forgotten to feed him.

I closed the folder and lifted it from my lap, but as I did so something slipped from inside to the floor. I picked it up. It was a song or poem of some kind written in a childish scrawl.

Do not Cry Baby Goose.

Mama Goose had a baby goose. Each time she tried to leave her in the nest baby goose cried so badly that Mama Goose was unable to concentrate on the business of fetching food and other duties.

One evening Mama Goose left Baby Goose to cry for one whole night. Oh dry those tears, said Mama Goose, do you not realise that I will come back?

The next time she returned she had in her possession a little stick doll fashioned into a goose body, complete with feathers and head, and a little bonnet just like Mama Goose herself.

Mama Goose gave the doll to Baby Goose and said, 'Now you will have me with you all the time, even when I am gone, so there will be no more tears at bedtime.'

Leah Goose.

A flood of new questions ran through my mind as Bertie jumped on my lap and began to rub his nose on my cheek. I resolved to put all thoughts of the orphanage aside for the time being, and after feeding Bertie I quickly washed, dressed, and retired to my bed.

There I allowed the darkness to draw me to its comforting void where I fell into an undisturbed sleep.

Six

Leah

My father's slurred voice echoed out into the hallway. The door to Mrs Featherstone's office was closed so I could not view how many people were inside, but I could sense that her voice was raised deliberately.

'There was no mention or demand of payment when you left your daughter here, Mr Cunningham. We are providing for her keep and giving her a roof over her head. In return she is assisting us by caring for the orphans. Every donation here is received via charitable organisations therefore there is no monetary reward or wages to be gained.'

There came some further words from my father regarding his rights and the payment of several shillings, but he was cut short again by Mrs Featherstone's stern voice.

'It is not appropriate for you to turn up and make unreasonable demands. I will have to send for the authorities if you do not leave this instant Mr Cunningham.'

The handle on the door turned and I quickly jumped aside to hide within the shadows. He emerged alone from the office, his head lowered, holding a familiar flat grey cap in his hand. Hit with a pang of nostalgic sadness, I held my breath for a few moments. Then I heard a shuffling of feet and a tap on my shoulder. I turned in alarm.

'Eavesdropping is a sin young lady. Please come inside my office so that we may talk.'

The guilt was evident on my face as I followed Mrs Featherstone into her office, engulfed with shame at the thought of my own flesh and blood committing such a lowly act. He would never have done such a thing prior to my mother's death. I had not expected to receive an explanation about my father's unexpected appearance at the orphanage, though I suspected that I was about to be delivered one.

'Sit. I have some questions,' she said in an even tone, clasping her hands together on the desk. 'I do not know how much you heard of the conversation between your Father and I, but I am sure you undoubtedly came to realise that he was here to profit from your services.

'I would like to know Miss Leah, why you think your father might be looking to acquire financial compensation. You know him better than I. How were the circumstances at home before you arrived here?'

I looked directly into her eyes, they were trusting eyes. I admired this lady a great deal. She was never overly strict but her face could change from soft to stern within moments. I decided I would open up and be honest with her, relaxing my posture before I spoke, though it was hard for me to dredge up such difficult memories.

'After my mother's funeral my father seemed to lose all sense of responsibility. He spent most of his earnings at the public drinking house at the end of each working day. A month or two later he returned home to tell me he was staying at the home of a Miss Elsie Cairn, who happened to be a middle aged lady with four young children that needed looking after on account of her husband dying from some manner of disease. Miss Cairn was the serving lady at the Tillers Arms.'

I paused, my breath caught with emotion.

'I am sorry to hear this but do go on…' she prompted.

'He spent much of his time between the Tillers Arms and our home each time looking all the worse for wear, until one day he came back to inform me that he had settled the last rent owed and was moving to Elsie's place for good.'

She raised an eyebrow. 'Did you accompany him?'

'No,' I replied, 'I was not wanted there at all, being just an extra mouth to feed. Miss Cairn had instructed father to take me to the workhouse, but it was full to the brim and so he brought me here instead.'

'Good heaven's child, that is a very heavy burden for you. We were not aware of these details. Your father only told us that he could no longer keep you both housed.'

I shook my head sadly.

'Mrs Featherstone please tell me… what did my father want? Had he only come here in the hope of some payment, did he not enquire upon my health?'

She shrugged regretfully.

'I do believe that remuneration is all he was seeking dear child. He made no mention of your welfare, or of seeing you. I am so very sorry.'

I lowered my head with remorse. I no longer recognised the man who had once held me tightly in his arms as an infant and sang to me lovingly.

The fact also remained that I had no idea just how influential Miss Cairn was to my father but it seemed that it was enough for him to rise against me, to view me as nothing more than a burden or someone he could extort. I was convinced that she had taken advantage of his vulnerability and poisoned him against me for her own personal gain.

'He was a good father to me once, he really was, Mrs Featherstone,' was all I could manage to say. I could find no fathomable way to explain my father's recent actions.

Her face softened again. 'You are a good girl Miss Leah and we are very happy to have you with us. Do not trouble yourself further over him. Let us hope that he does not return for the foreseeable future. In any case, my bold approach may well have deterred him. You, however, will have to decide whether you wish to have anything further to do with him. At this present time I fear it would only cause some enmity, especially regarding his bitter circumstances. I will do what I can to protect you but he is still your rightful guardian. I tell you that for now it is best that you do not fret over this incident.'

I nodded, her wise words resounding deeply. I knew in my heart that I could not reach my father whilst he was under the influence of the greedy serving lady he resided with.

I thanked my employer for her time and stood to leave but before doing so bravely decided to enquire upon Pixie.

'Mrs Featherstone, I was just attending to Miss Pixie after this morning's chapel service. I have been meaning to ask you if I could spend more time with her than is currently afforded to me.'

She looked up thoughtfully. 'Did Sister Ernestine mind you taking over her duty with this child?"

'No, she did not,' I replied. 'On the contrary, and if I may say so, I found Pixie to be relaxed in my presence. I fed her some broth and she ate many spoonfuls without making any sort of a fuss or acting in any disagreeable manner.'

She raised an eyebrow. 'Hmm is that so Miss Cunningham? Well I am impressed. The girl has been quite abhorrent since her arrival. I think Sister Ernestine might be glad to be relieved of her for a while.'

Assessing my hopeful expression she picked up her ink pen and scribbled on to some paper. 'I approve it, though you will be expected to provide me with frequent reports on her progress. She will be kept away from the other children for the foreseeable future, as we do not wish to frighten or disrupt the others. I will review the matter in a few weeks. Here is a list of items you will need for her care. They are to be found in the basement locker rooms.'

She handed me the paper and I smiled with gratitude. I knew that Pixie trusted me more than she trusted Sister Ernestine and I was delighted to think that I would have the opportunity to coach her out of the shell she seemed to have enclosed herself within.

'I will not let you down.'

'I know you will not Miss Leah, though do remember one thing. We are here for the benefit of all the children, no child is to be favoured one above another. I still expect you to fulfil your other duties and report to Sister directly on your schedule.'

'I shall,' I replied, curtailing my inner excitement in case she suddenly changed her mind, judging that I was already far too wrapped up in the welfare of the young girl.

'Oh and one other thing, Leah,' she said placing a hand on my shoulder as she escorted me to the door. 'Remember how I have told you that feelings always cloud our proper judgement? I want you to always be mindful of the degree of affection you submit. We do not know what the future holds for any of these orphans here. Their futures are bleak.'

She looked at me sadly and I knew instantly what she wished to convey. I nodded, though despite her comment I left the office feeling brightened. I even managed to put the matter of my father's actions to the back of my mind. If he was willing to disown me and try to use me for Elsie's gain, then I shall have no further dealing with him.

I could only pray that perhaps one day he would see the error of his ways.

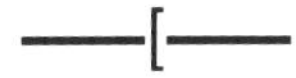

I retired to bed that evening in the hope that I would sleep more soundly than I had done over the past few nights. Perhaps I had lain awake pondering too much over Pixie Reinhart.

I would have asked Mrs Featherstone how she came to be immobile and resigned to her chair, but it would be far too imprudent of me to enquire on such delicate and private matters.

The facts, as revealed to me so far, were that the child was unloved and unwanted by her family, whomever they happened to be. I found it difficult to comprehend how they could not be lying awake at this very moment pondering her welfare.

I could relate to how Pixie must feel over the change in her surroundings and the separation from her family, though I was certain that much of her insular character had been brought about by the shock of her accident. Still, every child deserved to feel appreciated. I vowed to show her some degree of warmth and affection, despite Mrs Featherstone's disapproval.

I turned to my side and upon doing so I realised that Miss Jeannie was not inside her bed. It was unusual for her bed to be vacant so late for she often collapsed into it not long after her supper.

It was only Thursday evening. She was not due to return to her parent's home until Saturday where she would spend the weekend and return here again early on the Monday. I hoped no ill event had befallen her. My eyelids began to close involuntarily and I found my thoughts becoming muddled as I drifted into a slumber.

Just a few moments later I was fully awoken by a crashing sound and Miss Jeannie stumbling through the door in a state of exhilaration.

'Miss Leah! Miss Leah, are you awake?'

She giggled and I felt a thump through the floor as she fell onto her bed. I opened my eyelids. Her skin shone pale white in the moonlight except for the slash of red lipstick smudged across the corner of her mouth.

'Where have you been?' I asked in a tired whisper. 'You will wake up the entire building.'

'Oh hush,' she admonished. 'Why must you always be so dull.'

I frowned into my pillow. 'I am not dull, it is the early hours of the morning. Where have you been?'

'Not far. In the company of a very dashing young man.'

She laughed aloud.

I felt exasperated by her actions and hoped she could hear the disgust in my tone.

'You have been cavorting with a man until this late hour?'

'We have been talking, not *cavorting*. And he has asked for my hand in marriage. But of course I will not accept it, as I have two other suitors to contemplate first.'

'Did you kiss him?' I found myself asking imprudently.

'Oh Miss Leah,' she scoffed, 'you are so innocent in matters of love. Of course we have kissed. It is the very least we have done.'

I felt my cheeks grow warm.

'And do feel free to proffer as many questions as you dare, but I cannot answer them right now as I am to be up in four hours to attend to my duties.'

With that she kicked off her shoes and pulled the blanket over her head.

'Goodnight Miss Leah.'

'Goodnight Miss Jeannie.'

I closed my eyes. She could not be more correct. I was indeed innocent in matters of love. The very idea of feeling a romantic or passionate *love* with a person of the opposite sex was something quite alien to me. But she had stirred my curiosity with her bold words and I raised my head from the pillow a fraction.

'Do you love him? How does it feel? And how did you gain entry into the building? Doesn't Mrs O'Flaherty lock up every door and gate past eight?'

She groaned. 'Oh you ask too many questions. I only happen to know where she keeps a spare key.'

I laughed. 'You are so terribly bad.'

'Sometimes. But it is good to be bad now and then, is it not?'

'And why is that Miss Jeannie?'

She sighed. 'Maybe you will learn to be less dull and one day experience such a thing as youthful pleasure. Now go to sleep.'

I pondered her words and closed my eyes. We were quiet until nothing more could be heard except for the snores of Miss Jeannie, the toot of an owl, the high-pitched shrill of crickets conversing in the grounds, and the occasional sob or wail of a small child in the dormitory below.

It was a very normal night in the orphanage.

Seven

Annie

I heard the rain before I saw it. Thick heavy sheets poured forth from the sky to batter the rose bushes along the perimeter of the garden wall. The delicate cupped blooms bent over awkwardly, driven by the force of the wind which allowed the tips to kiss the sodden soil.

There had been a day like this when Pixie and I begged Mother to let us play outside in the rain and she stood silently at the window, pursing her lips tightly with disapproval, as she often did when we wanted to indulge in boyish activities.

'Little girls should not play in the rain only to soak their clothing and hair,' she would say.

Mother had no sense of fun or adventure in her spirit. Not a scrap of youthful playfulness existed inside her. I sometimes wondered why she had any desire to become a mother at all, for the bond of closeness which normally exists between a parent and child had never seemed to coil itself around the three of us. It wasn't even the case that she might have favoured one of her twin daughters above the other. We were just *there*. Children that were around her, or beside her, but never actually a *part* of her.

There was the occasion where she busied herself cutting up long thin lengths of colourful paper in order to decorate our home with lanterns for the celebration of her and Father's wedding anniversary. As much as we wished to become involved she would not allow us to assist in any way. I recall how we sat watching her a short distance away, our faces mired in disappointment.

She viewed us as incapable of being resourceful, that we might even enjoy creative pursuits. Instead, she preferred to have us sit quietly reading with our governess, Miss Tilda, and listening to the stories we had already heard a million times before. Stories which made Pixie roll her eyes and fidget mercilessly in her seat.

Father invested more of his time into our concerns but was often away on business engagements. We never knew where he had gone or when he would return, but we always delighted in pressing our noses to the window to see his dark figure walking up the pathway.

If we were lucky he might have acquired a small gift of a pendant, brooch, an angel delicately carved on to a teacup, or some other fancy item he might have picked up at the Harrods store in London.

At times, seated by the fireplace, he would place his pipe down on the table and clamber down on to his knees allowing Pixie and I to scramble onto his back. In those carefree moments Miss Tilda would tut and smile at the same time. She could not go above Father's actions and reprimand us, so instead she would stand close to the door in case Mother walked in.

Miss Tilda came from Germany, a place which was marked down in our schoolbooks and seemed a very long distance away. Her elocution sounded strange to our ears and Mother despised it when we copied the harsh sounding words.

She had a tight jaw and an ample bosom where she kept all manner of items, such as hair accessories and tiny trinkets. Her hair was a mixture of strawberry red and yellow yet always held back tightly in a conservative bun. Pixie and I watched her with awe one day when she plucked out two large hair pins and let her hair fall loosely over her shoulders.

She had appeared to me then as an angel might have done. I gasped and touched Miss Tilda's soft hair gently, lifting it to my nose and inhaling the foreign scent of a sweet spice, a fragrance I had never before known. She then laughed before quickly tying it back up to resume the more important matter of being our responsible guardian.

Our governess was not the staunch disciplinarian our mother was. She seemed aware that young children required flexibility, and occasionally the freedom to explore and run, unconstrained. On a few occasions she would allow us to remove our outer layers and climb upon the high garden wall where we often sat watching the birds hop from branch to branch. Or we would remove our shoes and stockings and run through the bushes which surrounded our home, the breeze lifting our hair. We performed cartwheels on the lawn and went about collecting leaves, berries, and other natural foliage scattered throughout the grounds.

Shortly before Mother was due home we would tidy ourselves up, step into our dainty shoes, and sit upon the large brown wicker chairs in the conservatory to continue sewing on our scrap pieces of fabric.

She appeared never to suspect a thing.

My parents were so very different from each other that it seemed quite unbelievable that they produced two identical children of a similar personality. Pixie and I had similar interests and desires and perhaps even similar thoughts. I knew and felt from my earliest recollection there was very little which set us apart.

Until the day we were separated.

My thoughts were interrupted by a loud knock on the door. I heard footsteps and then Mrs Byrne talking with someone in a hushed tone. A moment later she entered the room with a letter in her hand.

'It is a delivery for you, Madam.'

She handed a letter to me and I opened it. I could not recall any previous communications from the postmarked address, nor could I recognise the delicate sloping letters of the correspondent. I unfolded the paper within which was a rather plain handwritten note.

Dear Miss Reinhart,

Forgive my impertinence in sending you this brief introduction. I wish to invite you to a tea at my home. I once worked as an assistant carer at the Orphanage

Institution in Greenwich. It would be a great pleasure to meet with you.

Please RSVP at your earliest convenience.

My warmest regards,

Miss J Wakefield

I looked at the words, perplexed. Who was this lady and how on earth did she know about me? Did Miss De Bours or Mrs Stradlin initiate the introduction?

In my mind's eye I saw Mother's eyes turn cold and look away in flippant disregard, but her disapproval mattered not. That she and I were somewhat estranged made it somewhat easier for me to embark on this venture of discovery.

Perhaps it was best that I did not tell her.

I sat down at my writing desk with a view to replying instantly. I might be able to visit Miss Wakefield before my next sojourn to the orphanage, then I might be bestowed with further understanding and be able to formulate more meaningful questions there. My pen scratched the surface of the paper and when I finished, I quickly summoned Mrs Byrne to deliver the letter to the postal office on her way past the village.

I checked the clock. It was only a little after ten. Through the window I could see that the black streaks across the clouds had begun to move away allowing some brighter rays to filter through.

Perhaps a little fresh air would cheer me.

I could take a leisurely stroll and maybe even visit Mother. It had been over a month since I last visited. I found myself reddening with guilt at how easily I had put thoughts of her to one side.

I went about organising a few tasks then made my way into the village, posting the letter myself rather than taxing poor Mrs Byrne. My driver was not at my disposal that morning so I waited for the omnibus and thought about my mother's frail appearance during the last visit as I made my way to the station.

She had suffered six harrowing years since Father's death. I was afraid that she might never recover. The nervous breakdown she suffered shortly after the funeral had given way to relentless migraines causing her to become almost permanently bedridden, and little did that help as we were quite at odds with each other.

She disagreed with every decision that I came to. My most pivotal decision of using part of my inheritance monies to further my study in art was beyond her idea of 'usefulness' and she fought with me constantly over my choices, preferring that I use the money to travel to the buzzing capital of Paris, or somewhere where I might meet a potential suitor in order to settle down and wed.

It was not that Mother did not like Matthew, my fiancée of fourteen months, it was just that she could not understand the long term nature of our relationship, both of us choosing to put marriage to one side for a time in order to fulfil our occupational ambitions.

Matthew was extremely career driven, as was I. We had in actual fact entertained the idea of a wedding early the following year, which we agreed to plan during his weekend visits south.

The concept of an early marriage was becoming outdated amongst better educated women within higher accolades, though most in our circles refused to acknowledge this. It was not unheard of that some women were refusing to marry before they reached the age of thirty and looked towards fulfilling an educational role first. An ideology that my mother would never comprehend.

When the bus arrived I sat quietly in the rear. The journey was short, no more than twenty minutes long and I was glad of it, for I was eager to be done with the visit as quickly as I could.

The door was opened to me by Mother's day nurse, Bessie, whom she labelled an irritating *busy-body*. I was led through the air-less corridor to her room.

'She's been asleep for most of the morning and only stirred briefly for a bit of breakfast, but she should be awake by now,' she informed me before unlocking the door. 'Summon me if you need to.'

I peered through the door and found her sitting up in her bed staring vacantly at the thin-curtained window. The room was dark and held the strong scent of cleaning products.

She did not turn to face me as I stepped inside.

'Mother?' I whispered.

She glanced up and smiled.

'Annie my dear, oh my, how long has it been?'

Her voice was hollow and tired. Her eyes looked darker than I last recalled and her hair, now a peppery white, spread out over her bony shoulders which protruded through a thin white gown.

'I know, I apologise that it has been a few weeks but I have been so busy with my students.'

'Hush,' she interrupted me, waving a hand. 'You are here now. Sit down dear.'

I sat in a chair beside the window, wishing I had brought with me a gift of some sort, an offering that might ease the feeling of guilt I carried.

'How are you keeping Mother?'I asked with the usual formality we adopted between us.

She stared at her hands. 'Well my dear, all is the same, what else can I tell you? I *have* been taking my medication, though Bessie will probably inform you otherwise.'

'Bessie is only trying to do what is best for you,' I reminded her, as I always did, though her lack of appreciation in other people's concern for her welfare was something I had long ago gotten used to.

'Mother, I wish to ask you something.' I said out of turn.

She fixed a wary gaze at me, the weight of years of incompatibility hanging invisibly between us.

'It is about Pixie. I know that you do not wish to discuss her but, I think you ought to know that I am to meet somebody who once worked at the orphanage in Greenwich.'

Her face darkened and she closed her eyes.

'I know you disapprove, but...'

'Please tell me why must you continue to dredge up the past Annie?' She looked at me sharply, emotion shaking her voice.

I remained silent.

'Well?'

'She was my sister. And I have spent the last quarter of a century living with your pretensions that she ceased to exist.'

She scratched at her arm nervously. 'That is a lie, Annie. She suffered a grave accident. The sister you knew, and the daughter I once had, ceased to exist the day she fell from the garden wall.'

My body tensed.

'She might have fallen from the wall Mother, but after that both YOU and Father discarded her.'

Her eyes widened. 'No... no Annie! You don't understand the severity. She could not speak, she could not walk, she had left her body. She became a shell. The physician told us that there was no hope for her. She would never have a normal life. How could we live with that Annie? How could we wake up each day giving you the best in life when she required so much care? As well as the damage it might also have done to you. You would not have had all the privileges and the fortunate life you had if she had remained at home.'

I realised that I was leaning away from her defensively.

'You did not take me to visit her. Why not? Why for all these years could you not speak of her at all, do you not even care to find out what became of her? Do you know how she died, or even where her body lies now?'

I knew I was pushing her uncomfortably; her arms were turning red where she pressed her nails into her skin.

'They said that it was really for the best.'

'Who?'

'The physician. The staff at the orphanage. They said that we should cut all ties with her for any prolonged contact would be so much worse. Oh, enough of this, Annie!' she shouted, burying her head in her hands.

Footsteps approached the door and Bessie burst into the room with a look of disbelief.

'Have you upset your mother again, Miss Annie?'

'No, Bessie,' I replied flatly. 'But I do think it is time for me to leave.'

She glared at me as I headed for the door. 'Perhaps that is best then.'

'Please... Annie,' Mother called out, her voice trembling. 'You do know that I love you don't you? That your father loves you. Please know that we gave you all that we could.'

I shot her an irritated look.

Father *loves* me. She said the words as though he were still alive and able to feel the emotion. I left without exchanging another word, carrying a deep ache inside my chest. Whatever affection there had existed between us had been irrevocably damaged by my grief, hurt and indifference.

I knew that I should not have mentioned Pixie, or the fact that I was arranging to meet with Miss Wakefield. In my mother's mind Pixie had died on that tragic day. My hope that she might be more forthcoming about the details of her daughter and speak willingly was simply too unrealistic.

I caught the next transport vehicle home as quickly as I could so that I would have time to prepare for my class that evening. If I rested for a while I might even be able to conduct the session in a lessened state of agitation for I now felt an uncomfortable stiffness in my neck and my mouth was dry as a bone.

I stepped onto the bus and stared vacantly out the window. The sun was large in the sky with clouds spread purple and yellow like a thick bruise. My expression in the window's reflection was stony and my shoulders appeared hunched.

'You look just like her. Bitter and weak,' an inner voice jeered.

Was I to finish my days inside a care home the very same way? Would my fiancée return from his business trip to find a caricature of his former partner, a saddened and bitter old maid?

No! I decided inwardly. I was not like my mother at all. She ran away from truths. I faced them. The very fact that I was seeking to know about Pixie's fate was a testament to that. I would go forth with my intentions with or without my mother's approval.

Eight

Leah

I awoke with an uncomfortable layer of moisture on my skin and a dull pain in my head. Instantly I became concerned that I might be coming down with an airborne illness.

The mattress dipped and the tired bed springs groaned as I turned my body to one side and attempted to lift myself out of it, though I could easily have remained there much longer than my duties would have allowed. But I remembered Pixie and at once I felt a pressing need to go to her.

Miss Jeannie lay in an odd formless shape beneath her blanket so I decided not to awaken her. I dressed myself quickly then made my way to the kitchens for a hot drink and porridge, hurrying so that I could visit Pixie's room. Why I felt quite so terribly anxious to visit her this morning I did not know.

Along the hallway my eyes reacted negatively to the glare of the early morning light through the large windows and I held my hand to my face, worried that I might faint along the way. Each step seemed more difficult than the last as my heart thudded and my muscles ached from fatigue.

The door handle felt stiff in my hand when I unlatched it and when I walked inside I found her quietly tucked beneath her blanket. Gently I placed a hand on her arm as her eyelids fluttered open and she looked up at me with a hint of a smile. Contrary to how I felt, Pixie appeared well and eager to begin her day as she reached her arms up for me to lift her. I helped her to sit upright, tucking her legs beneath the blanket.

'Now Miss Pixie, after your breakfast we might take another walk in the gardens, though I do feel a little strange this morning, so you will have to bear with me.'

I glanced at the window and noticed the clouds were beginning to part though it was one of the chilliest mornings I could remember. I wrapped her in warm clothing, strapped her to her chair then wheeled her down to the kitchen to consume her breakfast, all the while avoiding any other person on my way.

Once we left the building and emerged into the garden I veered left and down towards the stream where few people visited. It was further west and meandered between tall bushy trees and the hard grey granite of the building itself. Heavy thick sheets of moss and lichen covered the side of the orphanage from this angle so that you could barely see the concrete structure beneath.

I adjusted the thick shawl over her head and noticed how the air was quiet as no birdsong could be heard. An owl hooted loudly in a tree close to us. Pixie covered her ears and her eyes sought mine nervously.

'It's all right,' I reassured her. I watched as her eyes then fixed upon a clump of nettles below her chair. She leaned her head forward to view something a little closer.

'Is it another stone?' I asked.

She let out a tiny breath of excitement. I picked it up and handed it to her. She stared at its rough edges and then dropped it on to her lap, leaning forward again to point to another.

'You want another?' I laughed! 'Oh my, I do believe you wish to start a collection.'

I searched nearby for a few interestingly shaped stones when I heard footsteps approach us from behind.

Sister Ernestine was walking towards us, her cheeks flushed with anger. 'Miss Cunningham, what are you doing out here in the cold?'

She stared at me disapprovingly with her hands placed firmly on her hips. I was about to utter some kind of an appropriate reply but she pointed to the building. 'And have you seen Miss Jeannie? She is not inside her quarters?'

I shook my head in confusion. 'But she was inside her bed when I awoke. I saw her. Though I did rise rather early and decided to bring Pixie outside.'

'Yes, but have you seen her since then?' she asked, wiping a bead of sweat from her brow with her sleeve.

'No.' I answered in all honesty. 'I left my quarters and did not think to awaken her.'

Her nostrils flared. 'Well I do believe she has vanished again, and where she is to be found only heaven knows. The girl is uncontrollable. Now her charge of children have been allocated to me and I am beside myself with enough duties. Why we allow these young girls to work here at all

I will never know for they are little more than children themselves!'

I stood silently and allowed her to vent her anger at me all the while wondering where Miss Jeannie could have gone. I did not dare mention the fact that she had crept into her bed in the early hours of the morning after cavorting with some young fellow within the orphanage grounds.

'Miss Cunningham, I insist you take Miss Pixie back inside and help us locate this wayward girl.'

I did as she bid, spending an entire hour searching many rooms where we thought she might be hiding, but to no avail. I resumed my duties then, checking on Pixie often. She still wore a healthy glow as she occupied herself with a set of wooden alphabet blocks.

Later that early evening, when I had retired to my quarters to take a brief rest and write up a few lines about Pixie, Miss Jeannie wandered straight into the room like some misplaced ghost.

'Jeannie!' I exclaimed, sitting upright. 'We have worried for you all day, where have you been?'

She slumped down onto her bed, a look of exhaustion overtaking her.

'Oh Leah, I am too worn out to talk, please just let me rest a while.'

I went over and touched her brow. 'You appear feverish. I must fetch Sister.'

'No,' she snapped, grabbing my arm. 'There is no need to cause her alarm. I am just a little weary. I will be fine after a rest.'

I frowned and placed my hands on my hips, almost emulating Sister earlier in the day.

'Why will you not tell me? Do you even care that we have searched much of the building today in an attempt to find you, just in case you had accidentally locked yourself into a room or suffered some trifling accident.'

She rolled away from me and mumbled to the wall. 'I was with Jack.'

'Jack? Who is Jack?'

She let out a long sigh and rolled her head to face me. 'Jack is my fiancée, I adore him, and no-one will convince me otherwise. I have been assisting him in the decoration of his new barn house where he keeps his wooden telescope. He will be the world's best astrologer one day you know? He is so very charming and clever Leah, I simply adore him.'

Her eyes misted over sentimentally.

I felt a pressing need to slap her. The petulant girl will surely soon be sent away, I was certain of it.

'That may all be well and good for you, but Sister is terribly cross with you now!'

'Oh?' she sat upright. 'What is new about that? Everything I do makes the old dragon cross. No matter what I do she frowns and complains. She has never liked me Miss Leah. She doesn't even like *you*! And you are the miss perfect new girl here who can do no wrong in Mrs Featherstone's eyes.

'Well let me inform you, Miss Leah, in case you didn't know, I never asked to be here at all. It was at my mother and father's insistence that I work in this bleak, cold, building with such unruly and bad smelling children and terrible meals that make me do nothing but retch!'

My mouth fell open in shock.

She turned to face the wall and waved a hand as if to be rid of me.

I decided to give up on Jeannie right then. I would tell Sister she had appeared, for it was only right to do so as we had all been very concerned over her whereabouts, but after her ungrateful outburst I decided I would have as little to do with her as possible.

In the large hall downstairs I found Sister Ernestine engaged in a reading activity with a large group of children. No doubt some were also Miss Jeannie's charges. She looked at me agitatedly. 'What is it Miss Leah?'

I whispered quietly in her ear. 'Jeannie is back. I have no knowledge of where she went however.'

She frowned. 'I will have stern words with her when I am finished here.'

I felt a sense of guilt creep over me though I decided to put it to the back of mind, and later that evening when I retired to bed I saw Miss Jeannie lying flat on her back looking upwards at the ceiling with a dour expression.

'Did Sister Ernestine speak to you today regarding your absence?'

Her eyes flicked over at me. 'Of course, though she will forget about it just as quickly. I will not let her run and control my life. I have been here an entire year and she has disliked me from the outset.'

I did not respond but instead penned Pixie's progress in the diary. We were quiet for some time until I found myself unable to let my true thoughts remain hidden.

'Miss Jeannie, I do not think it is right for you to be so mischievous with your private affairs. Can you not see Jack on your visits home, or the weekly dance?'

She looked at me as though I had grown a further set of heads.

'Why do you make such presumptions? Jack has no interest in dancing, and up to this point I have only been meeting Richard as a regular dance partner.' She sighed loudly as though I were some ignorant buffoon. 'Richard is the gentleman my parents approve of, but he is boring and does little to entertain me. I dare say he is even more dull than you. In any case I feel my heart is completely and utterly dedicated to Jack.'

With that she turned away and drifted into sleep. I felt sorry for her, despite her insolent manner and the sharpness of her words. I was clueless as to how she had managed to get away with her disobedience thus far.

I decided to turn my thoughts back to Pixie and my pleasure at her growing confidence. There were instances where she sometimes pulled away from me and showed a bold rejection towards my requests, possibly out of fear I supposed, but there too were many moments where I realised that she wanted very much to communicate with me.

I could not help but continue to wonder why she would not talk. She had suffered an accident, but she must have some recollection of what had happened afterwards, and what of her parents? Did they simply decide to discard her because of her disability?

Too many questions remained unanswered and though I was interested to find out what I could of the situation, my main objective was to offer the girl some sense of appreciation and a more worthwhile existence. Currently I had been able to entertain her as well as keep on top of my other duties, for if they failed to be completed I was sure Sister would curtail my association with her.

I hid my diary and trod along the corridor to her room. I thought she might have been asleep but I could hear a soft whimpering as I reached for the handle of the door.

I quickly opened it to find her curled up facing the wall. She seemed to be banging it with something. I rushed over to her.

'Pixie what are you doing?'

She held a stone in her hand. It appeared to have a sharp edge to it. Her hand was cut and bloodied. Panic engulfed me. Why did I foolishly leave her alone with such an item? I should have been more cautious, I still was not certain what she might be capable of.

'Let me bandage you up,' I told her gently. She pulled away from me as I reached for her. Then she began to shriek so loudly I stepped back in horror. She reached a hand towards me and I handed the stone back to her. At that she stopped crying instantly and closed it tightly in her fist. I stood beside her for a long while until she fell asleep then I slipped it out of her grasp.

I walked back to my quarters with the realisation that this child had suffered some terrible degree of pain and abandonment, something so upsetting that it rendered her young mind to become fragile and unpredictable. I looked up and implored the Lord himself, foolishly, as if He would give me an answer, for I only wished to know what it was that had caused this young infant to become so hurt, so unpredictable and volatile.

Whom had she loved and lost?

It was almost as if something had broken completely within her mind.

Nine

Annie

The first thing I noticed was the dainty row of buttercups amidst an overgrown tangle of weeds which spread along the entire pathway that led to the cottage's entrance.

Lowcroft Cottage had not been an easy residence to locate due to being situated between miles of farmland and valleys behind deep dense woods. I had very nearly ended up in a completely different location altogether and it was only when my driver, vexed with frustration by this point, enquired upon some local individual where Lowcroft Cottage was situated, that we were able to be on our way.

Thankfully the weather was agreeable on this fine day, and the sun warmed my cheeks as I approached the door where a simple carved sign which was hung upon it, said…

'Welcome to those who come in love and friendship.'

A nice touch I thought, or perhaps a silent message to warn strangers to keep away.

I knocked three times and the door was promptly answered by an elderly lady who wore a wide smile as she recognised me to be the person she had been expecting. She possessed a trim figure for a person of elderly years and her hair was the colour of cinnamon with irregular sprays of grey escaping beneath a tightly clasped bonnet.

'Do come in Miss Reinhart.'

'Thank you. Please call me Annie,' I replied and stepped inside.

The homely scene before me calmed my jittering nerves. A coffee-coloured armchair close to the hearth had ornaments of elves, fairies, trinkets and other smaller objects placed around it in a rather old-fashioned style of arrangement.

They each fought for my visual attention but my eye caught sight of some yellowing stains on the wall instead. I seated myself on the couch which also, if one observed closely, had a frayed edge down one side of it.

The flaws inside Miss Wakefield's well-tended home served to remind me of the cracks disguised within my own heart.

She relaxed into an armchair opposite, eyeing me from head to toe with a natural curiosity.

'I am very pleased you accepted my invitation. I had been unsure whether you would. May I fetch you a cup of tea or some other type of refreshment?'

'Oh there is no need to trouble yourself. I have only just finished an appetising breakfast engagement with my fiancée who is, as we speak, travelling back on a train to his destination some many miles away.'

She raised an eyebrow. 'Is that so? And what does your fiancée do, if it is not imprudent of me to ask?'

'Not at all,' I smiled warmly. 'Matthew is a comptroller for a large investment corporation.'

'How wonderful,' she smiled back, 'must he travel frequently?'

'Yes, I am afraid he must. And often. But we are quite suited to the routine, I have a very busy schedule with my art students, so our time together every alternate weekend tends to be of a higher quality than if we were together constantly, I feel.'

She nodded, making no particular remark, though I began to feel a little nervous then and touched the lobe of my ear. She must have noted my anxiety and steered the conversation elsewhere.

'Well dear, I did not mean to intrude into your busy life, but I had assumed that a meeting between us would be rather expected at some point, since we appear to have some sort of a connection, wouldn't you say?'

I nodded in agreement. I noticed how her face was indelibly marked by the passing of years, though seemed to also emit a youthful glow I could not quite describe.

'I must thank you Miss Wakefield, but I would like to know, how did you come to hear of me?'

She smiled, pulling her shawl tighter across her shoulders.

'I did not know of your existence until I recently visited the orphanage to deliver some charitable items to their office. I was informed you had paid a visit there just a few days previously. Of course I made the assumption quite irrationally, but am I correct in believing that you are directly related to the young infant who resided there many years ago?'

'Yes' I confirmed, wondering why Miss De Bours would inform her of my visit to the orphanage.

'She is my twin sister, and she was placed in the care of the staff there when she was five years of age.'

Her face took on a more serious expression.

'Alas, I do vaguely remember your sister though I am afraid that I do not know what became of her. That is something I cannot tell you as I left the orphanage long before she passed.'

Disappointment crept over me.

'I know that she passed away just a year after her admittance there but I do not know much of the details surrounding her death.'

Silence punctuated the air between us. She stared ahead without flinching, as though caught deeply inside thoughts of her own. I sensed a slight oddness about her manner.

A large clock in the room ticked away the passing moments, and I focused on the sound in an attempt to steady my nerves.

'Miss Wakefield I have found myself pondering her disappearance and death for many years. All I can tell you in blatant honesty is that she was taken from our home one very un-extraordinary morning. She had been playing in the garden whilst I was upstairs in my quarters. I heard a great commotion outside then I was ordered to keep away and remain upstairs in the care of my governess. I was told she fell from the garden wall and sustained a debilitating injury.

'She was removed from our family home within hours, and my parents, after a couple of weeks nurturing some privately held grief, practically refused to speak of her again.'

She shook her head. 'I am so sorry to hear this, but I can only imagine that grief can cause people to react in different ways.'

She looked away, but I continued.

'It grieved me so much at the time. I was not even certain if she had been killed or whether she was still alive following the accident. I was forbidden to talk of it. It seemed as though my parents wished me to erase her from my memory as quickly as possible.'

She frowned. 'Doesn't the memory serve to dredge up a bitter and painful experience that may be better for all if it were simply left to rest?'

I shook my head in disagreement. 'No. That I cannot do. The only reason I have not ventured into this degree of enquiry is because my mother is frail and suffers an acute malady of the nervous system. Any mention of Pixie sends her into quite a distressed and anxious state. I am afraid that she has never been able to deal with the course of events, and any enquiry I make upon her is met either with hysteria, or a heartfelt plea to desist from dredging up the past. Matthew too feels that it is not a good idea to do so either. He is very much of the view that I should lay the ghosts of my past to rest.'

She watched me, contemplating my words.

'But why now Annie?' her eyes seemed to cloud over. 'Why seek the truth about your sister now?'

I cleared my throat and stared at my hands allowing me a few seconds to formulate as pragmatic an answer as I could.

'Miss Wakefield it has been six years since my father passed away and I am coming upon my thirtieth year. In some ways I wish to unveil the truth before another decade passes. Also my mother is fragile and resides at a private residential care home. I can't help but feel strongly about discovering the facts and think she ought to be confronted with them before she…'

I hesitated.

'Before she passes away?'

'Yes,' I replied. 'I know it seems cruel but perhaps Mother and I can make our peace together once the truth is set free.'

'I see,' she replied. 'I can see why you wish to find out what happened to your sister but do you feel that my input is welcome? However vague or slight in detail it might be. I am afraid my mind is not as it once was, you know.'

She lifted her cup to her mouth with a slight tremble.

I spoke quietly. 'I would like nothing more than to hear it. It would be a privilege. And not just for the simple pleasure of unearthing any facts you can remember about my sister, but of course I am interested in your story in its own right, though, I do hope it will not cause you distress.'

She smiled but there was sadness behind her eyes.

'No, no dear. I think that perhaps a purging of the past will be a blessing, a great weight off my shoulders for it can sometimes be a heavy burden to bear. And so I will begin,' she said, to which the moment itself was marked by the clock beside me striking the midday hour precisely.

'I began working in the orphanage at the age of seventeen. My parents had been quite exasperated by my lack of focus and immaturity up to that point. I was a wayward girl you see, driven by the desire to please no-one but myself. And so they thought it was a good idea to send me there to assist the carers and learn the simple skill of obedience.

'I admit that even at that time I had no desire to be dutiful or bound to a service I was not made to enjoy. I have never really been the maternal sort of girl you see. But one does what one ought, and I can say to this day that I tried my very best.'

She paused to take a sip from her teacup.

'I believe it was in the spring of 1881 when she arrived. Your sister. A young girl with cornflower blue eyes, obviously hiding some sort of tragic fear behind them. A pretty little thing she was, but alas, I paid little attention to her.

'She was bound to an ugly contraption of a chair, one that had rusted wheels fitted to its legs and had been made to fit her snuggly and tie her securely to its back. She could not walk, though her eyes would follow you with suspicion, or stare vacantly away and not acknowledge you at all.'

I listened with deep interest realising that my mouth had rudely dropped open.

'Miss Wakefield, did my sister ever utter a word?'

'No. I have never heard her speak, though I recall Miss Leah made a good job of communicating with her.'

'Miss Leah?' I interrupted, recalling the name.

'Yes, our sweet and dutiful Miss Leah, who happened to become your sister's most devoted companion. Leah had joined the orphanage just a few months prior to your sister. She had come from a broken family herself, a deceased mother, and a wretch of a father that had abandoned her there.

'But despite her sufferings she had the fortitude of a lion. Nothing seemed to drag her down, though she was quiet, self-contained, and obeyed every rule. She was well behaved and generous in spirit, whilst I was the brash, selfish girl who liked nothing more than to run away and seek the company of the opposite sex.'

She looked away regretfully and stared through the window at the leafy ferns which bowed forward in the breeze, brushing gently against the glass.

'It is strange somehow, looking back. I can see how Miss Leah was the stronger one. The one with the most confidence.'

'Why do you think Miss Leah communicated so well with my sister?'

She gave a small shrug.

'I cannot answer that question Annie, it appears that some things are unexplainable, but Leah took to her immediately and somehow decided that she was to be responsible for the girl.

'Perhaps your sister's vulnerability or acute frailty brought out a willing desire in her. Who could know? But I believe, from what I witnessed in that orphanage your sister had known the truest feeling of devotion and affection during her short time on this earth, where many children in that orphanage did not. Even at their saddest moments they would hold on to a wanton wish for love, their frail dying breaths still bearing hope of a more contented existence. Surely all children wish for nothing but love?'

I lowered my eyes, saddened at the thought but heartened by the news that someone cared for Pixie.

'I apologise, Annie. Forgive me for steering the conversation so mournfully.'

'Not at all,' I replied. 'I have so many questions to ask you I did not even know where to begin. Though I do wonder, did my sister spend every day with Miss Leah?'

She looked up pensively. 'Oh yes indeed, they had some wonderful times together. I do recall that they visited the circus and returned in exuberant form. It was quite evident that they enjoyed it thoroughly. Much time was spent too with Miss Leah walking with your sister through the gardens on leisurely strolls. The happiness the two of them enjoyed in those moments was clearly evident.'

I smiled, warmed by the thought that Pixie had someone who paid her attention and cared for her, though I could not summon up an image of her strapped and immobile inside a chair, when my most dearest memories were she and I running through the garden excitedly, our hair flowing behind us as Governess Tilda chased us through the hedgerows surrounding our home.

Miss Wakefield was staring at me quizzically.

'You do not know it do you? You do not know why she came to be incapacitated. I can see it in your face. My dear you must be stricken with melancholy. Not knowing is often so much worse than bearing harsh truths. Didn't your parents love you both equally?'

I sighed. 'I am sure they did in their own way. Though mother was never naturally inclined to participate in our lives, well… not as a mother ought to. She was sensitive, fragile even, and any slight disturbance, or rise in our tone of voice would inflict a migraine or sudden bout of nervousness.

'Her malady caused her to retire often and she would leave us to our own devices. I know not what happened that fateful day. Pixie was in the garden and I was in our quarters. She suffered the accident then, for she was taken away and I did not see the result. My father said it would damage my mind if I dwelt on it. He forbade it. My mother did not speak about it and even now she…'

I looked away.

'She what?' Miss Wakefield prompted.

'Even now she cannot bring herself to speak of it.'

I shuddered as the facts tumbled from my mouth so easily.

'Whatever happened, she was paralysed, Annie. Of that we are certain.'

'But I feel it was wrong for them to discard her so cruelly.'

I bit my lip and tried hard not to lose control of my emotions in front of this kind lady. She leaned forward and gently touched my hand.

'It was their choice. You cannot persist in your private anguish over a decision that was not afforded to you.'

I saw sense in her words.

'I agree Miss Wakefield, but there is so much I feel I need to know.'

She glanced at the clock. 'Of course, and in that case you must visit me again very soon.'

I nodded, feeling slightly disappointed that she had decided to end the conversation there. I stood to my feet.

'May I ask one more question before I depart?'

'Of course,' she nodded.

'Is Miss Leah still alive and well?'

Her face paled. 'I am sorry to tell you that she is not, but I know where she is laid to rest, and it is very close to the orphanage, not more than five hundred yards to the east of the main chapel there. I believe your sister lies there too.'

She touched my hand gently and I noticed her fingertips were cold despite the room feeling overly warm. I smiled and bowed my head with gratitude.

I left the cottage knowing that I would not have the privilege of talking to Miss Leah about her relationship with Pixie, but an image of the two of them spending time together in the gardens surrounding the orphanage set my heart ablaze with a new-found contentment.

Ten

Leah

Sister Ernestine and I lifted the infants out of the steel tub of murky water and on to the thick mat which lay beside it, taking great care not to let their slippery bodies fall from our grasp.

I dried each one carefully, then pinned the small linen cloths between their legs as they wriggled and spluttered with tiny limbs outstretched and faces red with anger. We dressed them warmly and placed six in a row, side by side, into the long cot bed on the opposite side of the window.

They had all been recently orphaned, either from deceased parents or unmarried mothers who had breathed life into them but could not afford or find any way to raise them. They would grow up at the orphanage together, with very little being required of them until they entered a workhouse at a suitable enough age.

Sister said that more than half the babies in the orphanage did not reach the age of two years, as effective medicine was scarce and bouts and plagues of infant maladies took their lives very easily.

It took all my hardened resolved not to rock them to sleep in my arms for fear of developing a bond, though it broke my heart the way they had first screamed desperately for human affection.

But after three days they grew quiet, for they already learned not to persist.

Sister berated me whenever I picked up an infant and spoke to it softly. The babies were fed and put to sleep in their cots, no fuss was to be made of them, no matter if they cried or not.

'This is not a place for sentimentality,' she would say.

Miss Jeannie told me that she had paid a visit to check on all the sleeping infants early one morning only to find that two were a terrifying shade of blue. She had vomited in the latrine. It was a task she loathed to repeat, and so it was the irrepressibly stoic Sister Ernestine who mostly took over the task of monitoring them.

Once the babies had been laid to sleep for the night I retired to my quarters. It was a little after ten and I was alone. I had tried my best to avoid conversing with Miss Jeannie for several days after her insolent disappearance from the orphanage, writing in my diary at dawn using the sparse light that shone through the window. That way I could avoid disturbing Miss Jeannie's sleep. I still felt angered by her behaviour. How she got away with her secretive antics I could not fathom, and I could only conclude that her parents must have some good standing with persons connected to the orphanage.

I sat upon my bed and leafed through the diary entries now which filled more than eleven pages. They were mostly concerning Pixie's expressions of joy during our walks and her reactions to the things we viewed. The girl still refused to speak, though I was certain she could utter a word or two if she truly desired. It would just be a matter of time, as her trust in me seemed to grow day by day. I would issue patience with her and not press her to communicate.

I also made a note of how much she enjoyed collecting the various coloured stones and pebbles in the gardens where I cautiously made sure to discard any with roughened edges and hid them in her room before I left. Our walks had become a great source of excitement for her, though we never strolled away from the grounds. Not that it would have been easy to achieve, as a tall iron gate put paid to any such desires, though I would not be surprised if Miss Jeannie had mastered the art of scaling it.

I looked over at her bed, again wondering where she was and with which young fellow she might be frolicking with in the grounds this time. She appeared to show the most affection for Jack, informing me during our last conversation that they were saving funds to acquire a home for them both.

Stifling a yawn I realised I was growing tired of my thoughts and folded Pixie's diary away, snuffed out the candle and climbed into the bed to allow the darkness to draw me into its comforting depths.

It was then I was certain I heard a whimper. It seemed to come from the same room, yet there was nobody there. I stared upwards for a moment straining to listen and then it came again, a small whimper from the closet at the far end of the room.

I walked over and opened the door. There inside sat Miss Jeannie, awkwardly hunched over with her head resting on her knees, her russet hair cascading over her forearms.

'Miss Jeannie, what are you doing in here?'

She looked up and squinted. From the single beam of moonlight illuminating her face I could make out her tearful expression.

'I did not wake you purposely,' she muttered. 'I wished to be alone and not bother you at all.'

'But why are you in here?'

She shrugged. 'I am feeling very sad, must I give you an explanation?'

I sighed at her typically defensive response.

'Well come out of there at least and sit on the bed.'

She pouted like some unruly child but did as I asked her, lying on her bed to face the window which seemed almost prognostic with the amount of stars that twinkled across the sky.

I sat upon my own bed and watched her. There was something terribly sad about Miss Jeannie, but I did not wish to pry too closely for fear of her clamming up entirely. Eventually she spoke at her own will.

'I am very afraid Miss Leah,' she whispered. 'There are things happening to me, and I fear them greatly.'

'What is it you fear?'

Her eyes sought mine with the deepest desire for understanding.

'I have failed to experience my monthly course,' she whispered. The enormity of her words filled the room. I took a moment to register them, then my mouth opened and promptly snapped shut again.

'Oh Miss Jeannie, are you saying that...'

'Yes I am!' she cut in. 'That is precisely what I am saying. I think it is true and I do not know what I should do about it.'

Her chin trembled as she spoke.

'But... but you are unwed!' I reminded her.

'You are so clever Miss Leah,' she said, pulling a face.

I lay quietly thinking for a moment. I did not wish to upset her with any flippant remarks.

'I assume the father is Jack?' I proffered with caution, in case she would fly off the handle at such an assumption.

'Of course it is Jack. How could you think it is any other? And I told him that we should be cautious and not indulge in any adult relations until we are wed.'

'Oh Miss Jeannie but if he loves you surely he will marry you? Surely all will end well in that regard?'

She turned her eyes away. It was that moment that I knew that something else bothered her. Something she did not wish to reveal to me.

'How can I help you?' I said gently.

'You cannot help me.'

'But Jeannie, everyone will find out sooner or later, you must tell Mrs Featherstone. I am sure that she will try to find the best solution.'

'I cannot,' she insisted again. 'She will inform my parents and I will be shamed. That is all that will occur. You must not tell anybody Miss Leah. I will figure something out of my own accord. Please! Promise me you will keep this to yourself? she pleaded, her eyes two shiny black buttons in the pale light.

'Yes.' I assured her. 'I will say nothing, but please do confide in an adult. It is your only sensible recourse.'

'I have confided in you have I not?'

'I am not an adult.'

She shrugged and sighed, then covered her head with the blanket, a sign that she wished to speak no further on the matter.

I lay back and tried to sleep but my dreams began to venture into areas which disturbed me.

Firstly, my mother came to me with her kind eyes and gentle smile. She spoke softly, telling me that I was on a good and honest path and that she was very proud of me. In the dream I shed many a tear, for she looked more youthful and happier than I had ever seen her in real life.

Then my father appeared, he looked gaunt and bitter. I pictured him crying, for his life had turned towards an undesirable path. It was hard to believe how the circumstances of my mother's death had changed him so.

In the next part of my dream I saw Pixie again, but this time she was not in her chair but running through a field of buttercups, her hair glinting in the sunshine.

Then I saw another girl of the same age running just ahead of her. I was confused, it was hazy, perhaps the image had become blurred. I could barely see the second girl before the dream began to fade and just before she disappeared, Pixie turned back to look at me and I watched her stumble. I then had a rather uncomfortable sensation of falling which was so profound it jolted me awake.

The light streamed through the window and I sat upright breathing heavily.

Had I overslept?

I checked the clock and saw that I had awoken a half hour later than I was permitted. I jumped out of my bed and glanced across to see Miss Jeannie's body stretched out slovenly beneath the blanket.

'Miss Jeannie?' I called, but she did not stir.

I nudged the sleeping mound, but there came no sound or movement, not even the rise and fall of her body as she breathed.

The colour drained from my face as I peeled back the blanket to reveal only two pillows that had been carefully positioned to falsely emulate a sleeping body where Miss Jeannie herself should have been.

Just one hour later I was standing in Mrs Featherstone's office having been summoned there by Sister Ernestine after breakfast. I had told Sister that Jeannie was feeling unwell and needed a little longer to compose herself, but she just scowled at me and walked away. I was sure that Sister suspected that Jeannie and I were up to something secretive between us. This is how it must surely have seemed to her because Jeannie seemed only too happy to confide her troubles to me.

I had decided to keep my word to her however, and not reveal that she was with possibly with child. Nor would I mention that she had vanished from her bed this morning, stripping the entire closet of her clothing and other personal belongings.

These actions proved that she had decided to leave the orphanage permanently, perhaps to return back home, or to be with Jack. However, knowing the girl as well as I did, she might just as easily change her mind and so I did not wish to raise the alarm so quickly. It could be a few hours before her disappearance came to light.

I tried to put my worrying thoughts about Miss Jeannie as far to the back of my mind as I could.

'Miss Leah I am very pleased with the amount of care and attention you have shown in your duties. Your considerate and obedient nature has not gone unnoticed. I have a very special gift for you,' exclaimed Mrs Featherstone, extracting from her drawer an envelope and handing it to me.

I eyed it with curiosity.'Is this for me, Madam?' I gasped.

'Yes dear, take it.' she urged. 'Sit and open it.'

I humbly did as she asked and found that it contained two rectangular tickets, both stamped with a date and a large heading across the top.

The GREAT MAMMOTH CIRCUS &Vol 1 Fire Company -

Admit 1. - 1st March 1881

Trainers, clown, juggler, trapeze artist and sideshow.

My eyes widened.

'Is this for me? But the circus is this coming Saturday.'

'Yes, and you must attend,' she smiled.

'But why are there two tickets?'

She adjusted the spectacles perched on the tip of her nose to peer closer at the tickets.

'Look here, it is so that you may take your young charge along with you. This second ticket is for Pixie.'

I could not comprehend the kind gift which she had bestowed upon me and it took a few moments to register. I began to stutter awkwardly, 'But what... what did I do to deserve this?'

She shook her head. 'Come now, young lady. It is just a simple gift that is well deserved. You will attend the circus and take Pixie with you. May I say, however, that you must be on your guard implicitly with regard to her care. Though I know you are a trustworthy girl, I would allow you no more than two hours at the circus. Mr Hopkins will escort you there and arrange to meet you upon your return. During that time you will keep your wits about you and not talk to any strange fellows. Is that understood?'

I nodded. 'Yes Mrs Featherstone. I am honoured and humbled by your kindness. Though I do feel sad for the other orphans, can some others not also attend?'

She sighed deeply and sank into her chair.

'Miss Leah, we do not have enough resources to accommodate all the children, hence to blindly pick and choose who should and should not go would be quite cruel, I feel, therefore you should not speak of it to anyone else. Please do as I have asked and enjoy this rare privilege afforded to you, and more especially for the young girl within our care.'

I nodded and thanked her again. Then she pressed a hand on mine as I stood to leave.

'Have you received any word from your father by letter?' she asked most gently in order to allay any anxiety on my part.

'No I haven't Mrs Featherstone. Not since you talked with him last.'

'Ah.' she nodded. 'That is probably for the best. Go now, continue on with your duties then.'

With my spirits lifted I left the office and walked up the staircase with the intention of checking on Pixie, who by now would be waiting for me to arrive. I calculated that since the weather seemed disagreeable, I might spend an hour with her at play, where she could look at some of the brightly coloured tapestries and assemble the wooden blocks.

I had by now grown accustomed to lifting her out of the chair and gently positioning her between cushions on the ground. This method allowed me to sit close to her and assist her when she desired to lie down and play games. She sometimes enjoyed rolling on the ground which we did with great care.

I was halfway up the staircase when I spotted Sister Ernestine charging down towards me, her leather-soled shoes squeaking upon the shiny surface. Her sleeves were rolled up tightly and she carried a basket filled with stray items of clothing.

'She's gone again hasn't she?' Sister blurted out.

'Who?' I asked, knowing full well whom she meant.

'That wayward girl! Don't play tricks with me Miss Cunningham. She has taken all her belongings too. Do you happen to know about any of this?'

I stared at her for a moment feigning my best look of surprise.

'No Sister, I do not.'

I blurted the lie, even though I could not really find a single reason why I should do so. Miss Jeannie had hardly ever been an agreeable person towards me, or a close companion. If anything she complained bitterly about the orphanage, and took no interest in Pixie, also criticising my lack of interest in fashion or in attending any dances at the village hall. Yet I could not act maliciously towards her.

Sister Ernestine's furious glare now highlighted her lack of belief in my words as she charged right past me, almost throwing me backwards as she did so.

'Jeannie Wakefield won't be back here again if I have anything to say about it.' she remarked coldly before stomping down the remaining stairs.

I let out a sigh of relief that I would not be questioned further.

'I daresay it appears Miss Jeannie has no intention of returning here ever again,'I muttered under my breath, and as I continued on my way I felt a pang of regret and sadness for Miss Jeannie despite my mixed feelings about her.

Eleven

Annie

'Good morning' the gentleman shouted in a cheery voice.

I did not recognise the caller, yet I smiled politely as he walked towards me with his heavy boots crunching across the gravelled path. He wore a long black coat and I saw that he was a member of the clergy by the white collar fitted around his neck, perhaps even the curate in the small chapel nearby.

By viewing the deep-set lines on his face and the few remaining wisps of grey hair on his scalp, I would put him in his eighties.

'I bid you good morning Father,' I replied as jovially as I could. 'My name is Annie Reinhart.'

He held out a hand and I took it. 'Ah yes, of course. You have been here once already isn't that correct my lady? You may call me Father Mackintosh.'

I nodded and smiled.

'Yes, it was a pleasant visit and I am returning with a gladdened heart warmed today by the welcoming sun.'

He glanced upward. 'That is true, we have a rare break in the clouds and the promise of a blue sky if the remaining ones decide to part. Well now, may I escort you up to the main entrance? I am heading that way myself.'

'Thank you Father Mackintosh,' I replied.

We walked side by side where I could sense him viewing me with curious interest.

'Your sister lived here once I believe?' he said, unexpectedly.

'Yes,' I replied as casually as I could, 'she was my twin. I know very little about her I am afraid, save what I can recall as an infant.'

He raised an eyebrow. 'Ah of course, any memories you have must be somewhat vague, I'd expect.'

'Do you remember her at all?' I said, hoping he would not take offence at my sensitive question.

He stopped to think. 'I believe I do have a slight recollection Miss Reinhart, but not due to any personal encounters. From what I recall she was escorted about in a wooden chair attached to wheels. Just a slip of an infant she was, but alas, I travelled frequently in those days throughout the village and beyond so my memories are very hazy.'

'How did she die?' I cut in.

He stared at me, taken aback with my impetuousity. A moment's silence prevailed where only the shrill cry of a hawk flying overhead could be heard.

'She... well actually Miss Reinhart...' he stammered awkwardly.

'Hello,' came a cheerful voice a few steps ahead of us.

Mrs Stradlin was standing at the entrance to the building.

'Do come inside Miss Reinhart, it is a pleasure to see you here again.'

I looked at Father Mackintosh and he shook his head apologetically.

'It was my pleasure to meet you,' he said, before walking on ahead and leaving me in Mrs Stradlin's company.

We settled into her office. A rather uninspiring room it was, containing little more than a desk and filing cabinet as well as an abandoned stack of paperwork, which seemed as if it had been left there to gather dust for some time. A notion struck me that important administrative transactions must not move quickly within these institutions.

I was given the customary greeting and handed back to her the paperwork I carried in my case along with its original contents.

'Did you find the paperwork useful at all?' she asked me.

I looked at her directly, searching for a way to tactfully express my dissatisfaction.

'I am afraid to say I was rather disappointed with the lack of information, Mrs Stradlin. There were many papers but they appeared to have little to do with Pixie. Mainly lists of furnishings and items purchased for the rooms here. One note had several detailed drawings of her chair, and how it became assembled and disassembled.

'Some other minor details were included, such as the food products she consumed, but actually there was nothing of interest. No suggestion as to what happened to her at all. I wished to fill in these blanks for my own peace of mind, and I would like for you to help me if you can.'

She stared at me apologetically.

'Well I am very sorry to find that the information was not to your benefit Miss Reinhart, and I apologise for not being present when you first arrived here. Could I offer you a cup of tea and would you like to see the children again?'

I felt my muscles tensing. 'Please Mrs Stradlin, I am here to learn about Pixie. Is there nothing more you can find out? There must be something.'

She sighed, placing her spectacles on the desk and crossing her hands.

'I can only tell you what I know Miss Reinhart and it isn't much. When children die it is always a terribly sad occurrence. Are you sure you wish to dredge up the facts and go through those negative emotions?'

I took a deep breath. 'Yes, of course I do,' I replied, surprising myself with my words. 'The more I think about it the more I feel she wants me to. I have been having these dreams…'

'Dreams?' she said, raising an eyebrow.

'Yes, I think she comes to me sometimes in my dreams, and I feel much closer to her now than ever before.'

She stared at me oddly before speaking again.

'If you insist. Well, it seems that a dreadful tragedy occurred of which very little detail appears to be known. Your sister Primrose, or Pixie as she was known, was quite a difficult child. I believe there was some treatment, but nothing that could restore her ability to walk, and a chair was designed to transport her. I fathom that she must have endured quite some pain after her time spent in the hospital.'

She let out a long sigh as she scanned her memory.

'According to my research I believe that she was cared for well here Miss Reinhart, and there was one particular girl here, if I recall accurately, who seemed to take your sister under her wing. That particular young girl seemed to have gone to an extraordinary amount of effort to give your sister a more meaningful existence than she might have otherwise endured, albeit for a short period of time.'

Leah, I thought to myself.

'Your sister passed away at the age of six years, where I am afraid only the scantiest of details were recorded. I have one document here. I wished to leave it with you since I realised it was not in the same folder you took away.'

She handed me a piece of paper, yellowed at the edges.

I perused it with a shaking hand.

'She died from choking? On a small stone?'

'Yes.'

'But how could that occur, was she alone? Where did she get it from? I don't understand. How is that possible?'

She raised a hand. 'Please Miss Reinhart. You ask too many questions for which I do not have the answers. I am quite certain that it was purely an innocent accident. I can also tell you that there are many children who perish in a place such as this and choking or asphyxiation would have been a common enough cause. A quarter of a century ago, child-minding practices were not as stringent as today and infants would have indulged in all sorts of foolhardy mischief.

'Also take into consideration that your sister was of a very fragile nature, both mentally and physically. It is the overall consensus that she placed an indigestible item inside her mouth and it had become lodged inside her throat. We have on statistical record a great many number of deaths recorded as choking. Today those numbers are much lower due to better child management procedures.'

My shoulders relaxed slightly. I thought carefully about her words before responding for I had no desire to alienate the woman, though it appeared she was already becoming quite vexed with my persistent prodding on the subject.

'I know that she died at the age of six.'

'Yes, a good age for a child of quite some problematic and severe physical and mental handicap. We also believe that she became mute after her unfortunate incident. Voluntarily or otherwise we have no record.'

'Is there any other record of this, of the way she died?'

She reached for another piece of paper in her drawer. 'I checked for those details and there is just one other entry here. Look.' She passed it to me. It looked like a medical note. A highly illegible scrawl of which I could barely decipher.

'What does it say?' I asked.

'I believe it says that she tumbled from a wall of about ten feet in height. The injury caused paralysis to her legs. Her upper body showed some degree of movement, she could move her head and arms, but mostly the shock of the fall, and subsequent aftermath affected the poor child's psychosis. She suffered many fits of hysteria before almost withdrawing completely into her own world. How or why she fell is recorded simply as an accident.'

I blinked as I processed these words.

The memory of that day flooded into my mind, and each time it did all I could recall was the feeling of fear which flooded through me as my governess begged me not to leave my bedroom, for something terrible had occurred in the garden.

I stared at the paper and could not prevent a tear from sliding down my cheek. 'Oh do forgive me' I apologised, feeling sentimental and foolish.

'Oh not at all.' She handed me a handkerchief. 'Actually Miss Reinhart, the churchyard where she is laid to rest is very close to the chapel, would you like to see it?'

I dabbed at my eyes. 'Yes, yes, thank you. I would.'

We left the office and stepped outside to see that the remaining dark clouds across the horizon had parted to reveal a cobalt blue sky. The warm sun lifted my spirits as I walked behind her, attempting to keep up with her step. Her legs strode in a perfect rhythm as she walked with her hands deeply thrust inside the pockets of a long brown overcoat which reached as far as her ankles. She looked like a young schoolteacher on an outing, rushing on ahead to keep up with her children.

'I have not visited for some time, so I cannot confirm the state of the area I am afraid and I must return to the orphanage soon as I do not want to be missed,' she said apologetically.

When we arrived I saw that she was right. The concrete headstones which dotted the graveyard leaned in every direction. They reminded me of the crooked teeth inside an old beggar's mouth. Thick green lichen covered nearly every one of them, so much so that it was hard to read any wording.

She led the way past a gate and I followed.

'I am quite sure I have seen her resting area before, somewhere near that tree over there,' she pointed.

I could feel my heart thump in my chest as we made our way towards it and there beneath the drooping branches she stopped to look down at two pieces of rotted wood held together by rope in the shape of a crucifix.

'Here it is,' she called to me.

I held my breath as I walked over and saw that it was just a rotten piece of wood with a very faint outline of her name carved onto it.

'But there are no dates here, nothing at all?' I said in dismay.

She shook her head. 'They would not have had the time or means to put a great deal of effort into these matters. I am sure hundreds of children are buried here on unmarked soil. It is very unfortunate I know.'

I felt anger rise up within me. How could my parents not wish to provide their daughter with a decent resting place or a headstone fitting our family name? I wonder if they even cared at all when they heard that she had died. I tried to think back to when I had been attending a boarding school in Suffolk. Had Mother ever written to me to say my sister had perished?

I recalled nothing.

It was an event which went by unnoticed and unremarked upon. If I mentioned it to her now, she would likely succumb to another nervous episode and refuse to discuss it.

I crouched down and ran my fingertips over the letters. The wood was brittle and crumbling where the rot had settled in.

I am so sorry, I told her.

Mrs Stradlin placed a hand on my shoulder.

'Would you like a moment alone?'

'No,' I replied. 'I am perfectly all right and I have seen what I wish to see. I must thank you from the bottom of my heart for bringing me here.'

'It is my pleasure Miss Reinhart, I do hope that you will not feel too sad for the remainder of the day.'

I feigned a smile to hide the wretchedness I felt inside.

'I am perfectly able to manage, thank you.'

'Good. Well we should head back then. The sky is bright and I think the children could play outside and make good use of it,' she said before setting off through the overgrown path.

'Yes, of course,' I agreed, following behind.

On my way out of the old graveyard I wondered whether Miss Leah was also laid to rest close by and I made a mental note to return alone some day to find her.

I would make sure that fresh flowers were placed on the graves of both the girls.

Twelve

Leah

We had fortunate luck as the weather proved to be mild on the day of the great event. The journey there had not been too uncomfortable. Pixie sat quietly content. Mr Hopkins had kindly assisted in removing her from her chair and placing her on my lap with a blanket folded around her shoulders. The chair was laid vertically at the rear of the carriage and secured tightly with rope.

The carriage had made its way out of the village at a steady pace and the horse's hooves squelched loudly over the uneven and muddy paths and narrow lanes.

Finally we came close enough to see the navy and white striped tent in the distance. A metal pole in its centre pointed upwards. Already great excitement could be sensed in the air as a large crowd of people began mingling together, and a great booming voice could be heard announcing all the acts which had come from far and wide to perform that day.

Pixie's eyes grew alive with interest. She seemed not to appear distressed which had been my prior concern. I decided that I would not place undue pressure on her by joining the most popular tents and largest crowds of people, fearing that she might become anxious amongst the strange individuals.

We took in many sights and I talked to her softly, all the while telling her that every person here had come to see the greatest show on earth. All the animals had been trained to perform special tricks and that there was also a person with great skill who could balance himself upon a single wheel, and cycle across a rope from a very great height.

Her eyes became as round as saucers as she digested my words, though how much she understood of them it was hard to fathom. Once we reached the entrance gate, a man comically dressed in a tall hat, striped vest and odd long pointed boots bowed before us as our carriage came to a halt.

Mr Hopkins helped us alight from the carriage and we fastened Pixie securely in her chair. She held her cloth doll to her lap as we strode onwards, all the while I remarked on the sights before us.

'And there is the tightrope walker,' I said pointing to a dwarfish man who wore flat pointed shoes and yellow tights. He nodded as we passed.

We gazed in awe at the colourful scenery and laughed at the outlandish clothing that many of the circus staff wore; people who had obviously spent many years perfecting skills in illusions, magic, juggling, balancing and other imaginary tricks of the mind.

A fairly young boy, who I would put to be about ten years of age, appeared from a small tent enclosure and reached out to offer Pixie a stick that had colourful strips of paper at one end. She recoiled and he backed away a step.

'Aw are you shy, young missy? Well watch this, don't take yer eyes off my hand now,' he told her.

He produced a small container that was roughly the size of a matchbox. He placed it on his palm and tapped it with the long stick. Upon closing his hand he shook it, opened it again, and the box vanished into thin air!

I laughed and clapped and Pixie stared at him with intrigue. I reached into my pocket to hand the boy a coin. He thanked me, bowed low, and disappeared behind his tent just as quickly as he had appeared.

I walked on and found it hard to steer the chair over areas of slippery mud.

The circus seemed to be getting into full swing as people began to double and triple in numbers around us. As I stopped at one vendor to purchase two apples on a stick with a deliciously sweet casing of toffee, there came a young girl's high-pitched laugh behind me.

It was a sound I instantly recognised, and I turned to see none other than Miss Jeannie herself accompanied by a girl of a similar age.

A gasp caught in my throat as I cast my eyes down to see a small mound on her belly where there used to be none.

Her smile dropped as she caught sight of me.

'Hello,' I said, quite embarrassed by our sudden meeting.

She seemed stunned to see me there with Pixie.

I noticed how her hair appeared lank, having lost some of its pretty curl, and she looked weary.

Jeannie opened her mouth to say something, but was interrupted by the apple vendor. 'Whose next?' he said loudly. 'Come on young missy, there's a large queue waiting behind you,' he told Jeannie.

I stepped aside and took hold of Pixie's chair, glancing back one last time at Jeannie. She gave a small hesitant wave then turned away from me to purchase her apple.

I had been unprepared for the encounter, though I knew already that Miss Jeannie was with child. Mrs Featherstone had told me that her parents had decided she would not return to the orphanage due to an illness. Though she did not embellish me with the true fact of this 'illness' I presumed that Mrs Featherstone had been fed a lie or had chosen to be dishonest with me. I did not press the matter.

Miss Jeannie would most likely marry the father of the child and her life would become one of domestic servitude, something I predicted in my heart that she would come to resent. She was a free spirit. I could not envision her chained to a kitchen stove with hungry mouths to feed and a husband who was barely at home.

These new thoughts unsettled me to a point where I could not enjoy the remaining hour Pixie and I had left to enjoy the circus, nevertheless I painted a happy smile upon my face if only for her sake.

Finally, when Mr Hopkins arrived to escort us back I could not help but feel relieved. I had grown tired of traipsing across the field from tent to tent, and Pixie had fallen asleep with her apple stick still clutched between her fingers. It was all that we could afford to purchase.

On the journey back I looked up at the sky and watched it slowly darken with a thick belt of grey clouds. A single drop of rain splashed on to my cheek and I covered my head with my shawl. I prayed the heavens would not open until we returned and thankfully we arrived at the orphanage having narrowly avoided a downpour.

I left Pixie in her room and went about other duties, reminding myself to record the day's events in the diary. I wondered whether I ought to record the meeting with Miss Jeannie or not.

Sister Ernestine approached me as I fed two infants at the kitchen table. 'And how was your little circus excursion today?' she asked sourly.

'It was very enjoyable,' I replied, keeping my eyes lowered.

'Do you know what happened to Miss Jeannie?'

I stirred the porridge slowly, careful to choose the most appropriate response.

'I do not know, but I hope that she is well.'

'Oh she is well enough,' Sister laughed. 'She is with child. And the boy responsible is to marry her this coming week.'

I tried very hard to look surprised. I must have been becoming good at it for I had every cause to practice it often.

'Oh my. Poor Miss Jeannie. Well I am glad that she has his support.'

'I doubt that,' said Sister frowning. 'But she's a silly girl isn't she? I mean what a silly thing to go and do, especially with a boy like that.'

I dropped the spoon into the porridge and faced her.

'Like what?'

'Well, the boy she's marrying. He's already been locked up twice, once for beating an elderly person with a stick and another time after that for theft. Miss Jeannie will have her work cut out for her for sure. I would say her parents are none too pleased about the scandal anyway.'

I looked down at my lap for I could not think of a word to say.

She then took up the spoon and sat beside me.

'You can go now Miss Leah, I'll take over putting these two to bed'

I stood up and walked away feeling guilty. I should have spoken to her today. I should have waited and not rushed away. I did so because I was embarrassed to question her or ask her how she was coping.

Had I asked her perhaps she would have been open with me and I could have helped her.

But how?

It was not my place to become involved in her affairs.

I lay awake fretting that night, and when I finally did sleep sorrowful visions of my father returned. In the dream he continued to blame me for my mother's death, even though he had never done so in real life. He felt bitter that she had exerted too much energy on my welfare becoming frail and weak as her sudden illness snatched her life so quickly.

I tossed and turned over Miss Jeannie too and what might become of her and the baby. Would she see sense and refuse to marry Jack? And if she did not marry him, where would the baby end up?

Might the infant even end up here?

I awoke with a feeling of dread and the sheet beneath my body became drenched with perspiration. I opened my mouth to speak but found that I could not. My throat had somehow grown swollen in the night and I tried to utter a word but could only emit a painful croak.

Had I caught a terrible dose at the circus the day before? It was only when I managed to drag myself to the kitchen that the Cook caught a look at me as I crouched over my bowl.

'Oh dear,' she remarked, grimacing. 'Looks like you have had better days Miss Leah, best get straight back to bed with you before we all end up in the same boat.'

Thirteen

Annie

The call arrived at six pm. I placed the receiver to my ear and listened half-heartedly to a litany of complaints.

'She is not responding to me... she refuses to eat... her breakfast lay untouched this morning... did you upset her again Miss Reinhart...?'

It was so redolent of every past visit I had ever made that I could not help but roll my eyes. It was always about *her* and the beacon of pity which she shone upon herself. She had to be the frail one, the pitied one, never I.

I replied to the nurse vaguely, promising her that I would soon visit with a fresh bouquet of flowers plucked from the garden, and as always, that would suffice for a while. I needed to say nothing more for Bessie already knew well the dire situation between us. It was her duty to report Mother's well-being should there ever be any sudden or swift decline in her health, but there was nothing either of us could do to change her mood, we simply had to accept the ebb and flow of her incalculable actions then wait patiently for her disposition to improve.

I wondered whether bringing up the subject of her ghostly daughter again had been a foolish miscalculation on my part. She would never open up to me and that was simply how it would be until the very day her body was laid to rest.

Additionally, there had been nothing revealing in the paperwork concerning how my parents handled the whole affair. I was disappointed with it all.

If truth be told, my mind now swayed to the subject of Leah Cunningham. I was curious about who she was and the role she had played in my sister's life. As forthcoming and amiable as Miss Wakefield was, I found her stalling in her words frequently, as though there were details she did not wish to provide or seemed intent on holding back.

Perhaps on my next visit, I could be more open about my own life and that might ease and relax her enough to do the same. I could not put my finger on an arbitrary feeling that she had stirred within me.

I switched on a desk lamp in the study and settled in a chair with a cup of freshly brewed tea. I caught sight of the ornately framed photograph of Matthew and I, one taken on a balmy evening during a weekend trip to Cornwall, his contented smile frozen in time as I stood close to him, my arm locked inside his.

I had pushed all thoughts of him aside in recent days and I hoped that he did not notice my indifference during our last meeting together. I was concerned about his forthcoming arrival too, and confessing about my orphanage visits. I was certain he would frown at my behaviour, for the last time I touched upon the subject he remarked that whatever the outcome was to be, it would do little more than cause unnecessary grief and play on my nerves.

I swiftly turned the photo to face the wall, selfishly putting thoughts of him to the back of my mind once again. I had no classes scheduled that evening and so I decided I would read for a while before retiring to my bed.

Just as I leaned over to collect a newspaper from the side table I spotted two small pieces of paper poking out from beneath the armchair. I picked them up and viewed them closer.

I am so sorry Miss Leah. I did not wish to upset you. But I must marry him.

J

I sat staring at the words for some time trying to find some meaning behind them. Had Leah tried to prevent a person from marrying? It seemed a very serious situation in any case. I folded the note and put it aside. I then looked at the other which had been written more formally.

I spoke to her this morning. Sister reported her as unresponsive in the aftermath. I fathom that she was not upset at our decision. She will be sent to the alternative place of residence in two days.

Mrs Matilda Featherstone –Institutional Secretary

Certainly it appeared that whatever had occurred it had been eventful enough to give someone their marching orders. Was it Leah or Miss Wakefield? It dawned on me then that I had no knowledge of Miss Wakefield's full name. A feeling of stupidity washed over me. I decided I might deliver the notes to her, perhaps she could shed some light on the matter, for surely she would have known who had been released from their duties at the very least.

I heard the patter of raindrops on the window and stood up to close the curtains. Bertie followed me to bed and together we settled there. I stared up at the ceiling as though it might somehow reveal answers to me directly. Finally I drifted into sleep, but I spent the night tossing and turning, dreaming of Pixie and an image of her came to me as she might have looked strapped inside her chair with a young girl standing behind her.

The girl pushing the chair looked determined and fearless.

Round and round the orphanage grounds they went together as she told Pixie stories about her own life, stories that I would never come to hear.

Then the vision seemed to turn quite dark. I found myself walking through the wide bleak corridors inside the orphanage itself, where children passed me with tear-stained cheeks. I asked one little boy where Pixie was but he shrugged and ran away without responding.

I continued onwards, up two or three curving flights of stairs to a door I was sure I had not visited before. I turned the handle but it was locked. Inside came a whimpering noise, a child like cry that startled me as I rattled the handle in an attempt to gain entry.

A cold chill swept through me as I heard the thunder roar outside and footsteps coming along the hard wooden floor. The sweet sound of a choir of children singing Christmas songs could be heard faintly in the distance.

The whimpering abruptly stopped and I felt a cold hand touch my arm. I jumped with fright and turned around to face the same girl who I had seen pushing Pixie through the grounds. But now she was not laughing, or talking excitedly. Her face was red with fury and her chest thrust outwards. She seemed ready to explode with a pent up anger.

"It's too late... You are too late... We cannot save her!" she screamed at me above the loud claps of thunder.

I bolted upright in my bed, gasping for air. A layer of perspiration had soaked through my nightdress completely. I felt I could not breathe in that moment. Thankfully it was only a terrible nightmare but I could not rest again. Instead I lay in the dark, trembling with a restlessness that prevented further sleep, fearful that I should happen to meet with the same unhappy spirit I came upon.

After moments had passed I rose and visited the study. There I sat at the desk and drew out a clean sheet of paper. I began to write and when I had finished, I placed the note inside an envelope.

It must have been much later than I realised, as very soon the first light of dawn penetrated the curtain and cast a soft light across the room.

Fourteen

Leah

'Miss Leah, you must sit up and eat.'

I recognised the speaker but I was groggy and unsure as my mind swirled and dipped with confusion. After a moment or two had passed I tried again to focus on the blurred image in front of me until finally Sister Ernestine came into view. She held a bowl of broth in her hands and looked down at me with concern.

My throat burned.

I grimaced and tried to swallow.

'Let me help you,' she said, placing a hand behind my head and lifting me upright.

'What happened to me?' I asked in a low mumble.

She stirred the broth slowly. 'Well Miss Leah, it seems you passed out with pain and you've been delirious for days, but thank heavens the fever has subsided now. You'll have to remain in bed for a while longer.'

I gripped the bed sheets.

'Is Pixie all right?'

'She looked away when she spoke. 'She isn't eating much, but then...'

I threw the blanket aside and began to stumble towards the door.

'I must go to her.'

'Miss Cunningham, you must remain inside your bed until you are healed. Do you wish to pass your ailment on to others?'

'Please,' I croaked. 'I promise to return to my bed. I must see her.'

She studied me for a moment then waved a hand in resignation.

I scurried along the hallway as fast as I was able to, my throat still burning with pain. If Pixie was refusing to eat it was because she must believe that I had abandoned her.

I prayed she would forgive me.

When I unlatched the door and entered I saw that she had been positioned beside the window. She looked sullen as she tapped the glass with one finger. The healthy glow to her cheeks had gone and now her skin looked pale and her eyes dull.

She caught sight of me and began to cry.

I held her close.

'I am so sorry,' I said, and she touched my cheek as though she could not believe that I had really appeared.

'I succumbed to a dreadful illness Pixie. But the worst is over and I will be perfectly well again now, you shall see.'

She placed a thumb in her mouth and began to suck it, resting her head with its soft fine hair on my cheek.

We remained like this for a few moments until I heard a growl in her belly.

'You must eat your porridge like a good girl for Sister today or shall I be terribly disappointed,' I told her.

I then returned to my room to see that Sister had left the broth at my bedside. I attempted to swallow a few spoons; my body thankful for the nourishment. Afterwards I decided to write inside the diary which was still hidden beneath the mattress. I wrote about my illness and a few other observations that I had made in the last few weeks concerning Pixie's progress.

The circus trip, for example, where Pixie had loved watching the elephants raise their trunks with the bright coloured balls balanced on top of them. They had circled the dusty arena in perfect synchronisation, not once missing a step or falling out of rhythm with the accordion player who serenaded them along.

When they let the balls fall she had let out an excited giggle until one bellowed and trumpeted so loudly she became alarmed, and placed her hands over her ears and closed her eyes tightly.

I turned to a new page and wrote the following:

Pixie can understand what I tell her and each day she becomes more responsive. She does not always obey my command and there is room for improvement. She still enjoys collecting small stones found near the stream. Particularly her eyes will spot semi-transparent glassy rocks that glint prettily in the sun.

She is inquisitive, playful, and it is clear that the

changing seasons and the beauty of nature has had a positive effect which brings out a calm placidity that can be both seen and felt inside her.

Her cheeks glow and her health is of a better condition than when she first arrived here. She does not seem to be put off by the cold or the rain but enjoys feeling the cool drops of water on her skin.

Due to my illness she has been left inside her room for some time. I see a change in her already. I can only thank the Lord that I am recovered and can resume my care, for she has missed my presence.

I hesitated, thinking I ought to stop there, but continued on...

Miss Jeannie attended the circus too. She seemed just as surprised to see me as I did her. When I stood to one side and viewed a certain angle of her I could see the protrusion of her stomach revealing that she was with child; her own fear that had come to pass.

I did not speak to her, nor did she approach me, as the vendor of the stall stole her attention and I took hold of Pixie's chair and moved on.

I wonder what might become of her. I saw no wedding band on her finger. I should pray for her, for she was not always clear or certain about her desires.

In any case, I do hope that the child is born in good health and that Jeannie has a supportive ally in Jack. If what Sister told me about him is true, I do hope that he has (or will) change his ways for her sake.

It hurt me to see how sad Pixie became in my absence and so I penned a story about a goose who required to leave its own young in order to hunt for food. I would read this to her before bed so that she might understand that I would never leave her permanently. Never *willingly*. I would resist and avoid that ever happening.

A tear slid down my cheek as I recalled Miss Jeannie. I also cried for my poor mother who I wished was still alive, but I knew that it would have been far worse if she was. My father was no longer the caring and responsible person she had known. She would surely feel anger and disgust if she saw him now.

Father had not returned to beg money from my services, and for that I could be thankful. I swallowed hard and slid the diary deep under the mattress again. It was then I looked up to see Mrs Featherstone in the doorway watching me with a forlorn expression.

I stood upright and was about to speak but she held up a hand to silence me.

'Miss Leah, I have some sad news.'

She then entered the room and I climbed back into my bed fearing the worst, certain that my days at the orphanage were about to come to an end.

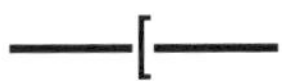

The hospice in Bermondsey had a fixed rotation of seven nurses who lived in the premises and cared for the sick patients which resided there.

This information was provided to me by Sister Ernestine as I ate my breakfast silently the morning after Miss Jeannie's tragic event reached my ears. I had been shocked when Mrs Featherstone informed me that Jeannie had been found unconscious in her home. There had been a terrible bleeding and she was taken to the local hospice, the baby all but lost.

As if the news about her miscarriage was not upsetting enough, Sister made a point of expressing her own opinions about Miss Jeannie's family.

Miss Jeannie, she said, had parents of less than desirable qualities and so it was no surprise that she had come to such a terribly unfortunate predicament. The girl had likely miscarried her baby because she had been spoiled, badly educated, and her parents could only be blamed for allowing her to take up with an equally uneducated fool to begin with.

That was the truth according to Sister Ernestine, and it would have been futile to argue with her.

It did seem to me that Sister, as opinionated as she was, seemed to know the background and inner workings of most of the villagers in the area, which seemed surprising to me since she only left the orphanage once a week to indulge in a shopping expedition within the main village.

As it conveniently transpired, that Saturday morning she was to partake in an excursion into town, and so Mr Hopkins kindly agreed to transport me to the hospice close by so that I may visit Miss Jeannie.

I admitted to myself that it would feel a little awkward, especially as we did not part as good friends or even on good terms. Nonetheless, I hoped that she might be cheered by a visit from someone who would not judge her or make her feel guilty regarding her situation.

After breakfast I sat patiently at the back of the carriage awaiting Sister Ernestine. When she did finally appear, I saw that she was wearing a gargantuan hat decorated with fruits. It was a style of hat I had never been privy to witnessing before and so I had great difficulty stifling a giggle.

Mr Hopkins, a genteel man of few words, rolled his eyes and glanced back at me with amusement.

It appeared that she had also replaced her starched white apron with a frock of strangely large proportions and patterned with flowers of an unidentifiable species.

Quite frankly, I thought that Sister Ernestine looked much like an advertisement for an annual flower show, and Mr Hopkins looked as though he might soon be unable to contain himself from bursting into laughter.

She reached the side of the carriage and lifted a high booted leg into the hoister with a determined agile swing, only to dangle there for a moment with her bottom end in full view as she raised herself onto the carriage.

Mr Hopkins snorted.

Sister then settled herself comfortably and I was thankfully left in peace as she opened a book and began to read at a marked page.

Soon enough I was released at the hospice just a few kilometres away.

When I first set my eyes upon it, the building appeared rather characterless. A bland and lifeless exterior had been half-heartedly adorned with wilting flowers inside plain wooden crates.

I entered and was taken aback by the pungent and musky smell of aged furniture and spoiled food. Along the windowless corridors it struck me that many of the patients appeared to be more mentally anguished and lacking in personal hygiene, than suffering physical disabilities.

One elderly lady plucked furiously at her matted hair as if she were trying to pick out fleas. Her face was covered in open sores and when I smiled at her only two blackened teeth smiled back.

I found Jeannie in a small room at the end of the main corridor. She lay face up on a bed with her hair spread untidily over her shoulders. Her frailty took my breath away, for she appeared at least ten years older than her true age.

She opened one eye and looked at me warily.

'I am so sorry,' I said, close to tears.

She blinked, reached out an arm and touched my hand. I spotted a dark purple bruise on her forearm.

'Please, will you come back to the orphanage?' I said impulsively, then wished that I could retract my words.

She shook her head.

'I cannot Leah, you know that I love him.'

I looked down at my lap. 'Are you still going to marry him?'

I saw that there was no wedding ring on her finger.

'Yes,' she whispered.

'Jeannie,' I said, taking hold of her hand. 'If Jack did this to you, please do not marry him. You can come back to the orphanage, you can begin all over again. Mrs Featherstone will allow you to return. Honestly. I can speak to her on your behalf and you will...'

'Leah stop,' she objected. 'I cannot come back. I am far too ashamed. Anyway this tragedy was all my fault.'

I squeezed her hand. 'How? How is it your fault?'

Her eyes searched mine for understanding.

'I was awful to Jack. I... I had screamed at him and beaten at his chest and he had gotten so cross with me. I persisted in telling him that I would refuse his proposal. He was right to react in the manner in which he did. But he is now sorry, he has promised me that he will never raise a hand to me again.'

I pulled my hand away and stood to my feet.

'You have lost your precious baby Miss Jeannie. It was *him* that made you lose it, but you are blinded by your feelings. Think about that!' I snapped.

'Feelings?' she spat back. 'You dare to accuse me of such a thing when you cannot survive a few hours alone without your precious little orphan girl! Well, she will never walk or talk, Miss Leah. She will never be what you want her to be, no matter how much you try to love her.'

In that moment I felt as though my heart had stopped beating.

She turned her face to the wall.

She was finished with me.

Nothing more could be done to dissuade her from making a dreadful mistake. Her spiteful words had cut me sharply.

I left, saddened that the visit had done nothing but deepen the tensions between us.

Outside, the rain washed the tears from my cheeks. It was a hard thing to do, leaving Jeanne alone in her bed of lies and deceit. Nothing I said, or did, would change her mind. I could not see how she could marry such a wicked person and I feared that nobody else would try to stop her.

I made a mental note to speak to Mrs Featherstone about it, maybe she could intervene. Perhaps talk to her parents, though at this very moment everything seemed futile.

Mr Hopkins sat in the carriage with a hat pulled low over his ears, puffing on a thick cigar. He seemed surprised to see me so soon and I made some excuse about Jeannie being asleep.

Poor Mr Hopkins had been put out of his regular duties to escort me, and for that I was grateful. I only hoped he did not notice the anguished look upon my face as we set off.

Once my temper had cooled I felt nothing less than wretched for running off and leaving Miss Jeannie though her words had cut into my heart. I sat sulking in the carriage as we travelled, admonishing myself for my actions. I then realised that it would do me no good to brood over the situation and tried to direct my thoughts elsewhere.

Soon enough the carriage turned into the familiar grounds of the building and stopped at the entrance. There I saw another carriage parked a short distance away with a driver waiting inside it.

There was a visitor.

It was rare to see anyone other than a physician, nurse, or the usual supply delivery cart which made its way a few times a week from the main village.

I decided that I would check on Pixie, and hurried up the stairs and down the long familiar hallway to her quarters. Just as I was about to open the door I heard a gentleman talking inside the room. I froze. I could not make out what was being said so I pressed my ear to the door.

It was Mrs Featherstone's voice now.

'Honestly Mr Reinhart, if she does not wish to respond to you perhaps it is better to let her be.'

Mr Reinhart?

I wondered whether I should knock politely or return to my room and visit again later, but then the handle turned and Mrs Featherstone emerged with the gentleman close behind her.

'Ah, here she is. Well Miss Leah I did not expect you back so soon. This is Pixie's father. He is paying a brief visit.'

I looked up at him and curtseyed. He smiled but I saw that his eyes were sad.

'I was just telling Mr Reinhart that Pixie is doing so well in your care, isn't that so?'

'Yes,' I replied, unsure how to respond as my heart hammered loudly in my chest.

Mr Reinhart nodded and turned away.

Perhaps he felt ashamed at leaving his daughter here and did not wish to indulge in conversation.

'Well, thank you both,' he said rather nervously then tipped his hat and continued on. Mrs Featherstone raised her eyebrows at me and followed him.

I entered the room and found Pixie at the window looking quite agitated.

Had she been unsettled upon seeing her father?

She turned her head and lifted her arms. I took hold of her and rocked her.

'I am back. I am sorry that I left you alone but I had something I needed to do.' I brushed the hair from her face and tilted her small chin up to face me.

'Shall we go outside after lunch is served? Would you like that?'

She gave a tiny nod and I strapped her into her chair to escort her to the kitchen. I could not know what happened with her father but it seemed clear that she had been unresponsive, even disinterested in him.

Why did he look so sad?

And if Pixie's father was able to visit his daughter why did her mother not visit also?

I made a mental note to further explore these questions in my diary, or perhaps I might find the courage to ask Mrs Featherstone herself, but more than that, something new dawned upon me.

I had become something of a mother to this young child. Or perhaps more of a sister.

Yes, I was a sister.

For I was too young to be a mother, even though my fifteenth year was fast coming upon me.

Pixie relied on my presence, and it was clear to everyone at the orphanage that she did not much care for the companionship of others. I had gone ahead and done what the staff had warned me not to do.

I had become emotionally attached.

The silent enormity of that situation weighed on my shoulders so heavily that I could barely prevent myself from wiping tears from my face for the rest of that afternoon.

Fifteen

Annie

Miss Wakefield poured out a second cup of tea. I had already been at the cottage for most of an hour sipping at the beverage impatiently.

She seemed bright and clearly in a talkative mood. I nodded agreeably as she attempted to educate me, with some greatly vested interest, on her local Suffrage Alliance affairs.

As she filled me in on the finer details she set the iron kettle down on the stove and returned to her chair. I noticed a slight limp in her gait, something I did not recall from my last visit.

She brushed away a sleepy white cat that had curled itself up on her seat. It seemed none too happy to be dislodged from its position until she picked it up gently and set it down on the ground at her feet, then heaved herself down with a relaxed sigh.

'I must say I am delighted that you contacted me again Annie. I do not get many visitors these days. It is always a pleasure to see a friendly face.'

I lifted the teacup to my lips and smiled. 'Actually, I have brought something to show you. I hope you do not find it too imprudent of me but it did raise a little curiosity when I discovered it.' I took one of the paper's from my purse and handed it to her.

As she read the words her expression darkened.

'Oh Miss Wakefield have I upset you. I am so sorry, it was not my intention at all.'

I felt suddenly wretched. What memories must I have stirred within her?

She held up a hand. 'No it is quite all right. Where did you find this?'

'It was contained within a folder given to me at the orphanage which held some of my sister's documents. It is only through mere curiosity that I thought of showing it to you.'

She appeared suddenly uneasy and I noticed that her hands trembled slightly as she began to explain.

'It was not a great surprise that Leah was angry with me. Yes this message is one which I forwarded on to her following her visit to the hospice. I had miscarried a child, you see. I had been beaten black and blue by the boy I had hoped to marry.'

She lay the paper beside her on the chair and stared at it.

'Since leaving the orphanage Jack and I moved to a place not too far from here. We had every intention of making a home for ourselves and the new baby. Though now when I look back at it all, I am not even sure I could call it a home, it was more of a crumbling shack but we made the best of it.

'My parents had been very disappointed that I was with child and my father turned away from helping us at all, deciding that Jack and I should be left to our own devices.'

She paused to remove her glasses and wipe her brow.

'Anyhow, it was not long before things took a turn for the worse. I seemed to suffer awfully from morning sickness. I couldn't eat very much and it left me quite exhausted and bed bound. I waited terribly long hours for Jack to return and assist me, but he would arrive very late, long after his working hours had ended.

'When he did walk in, he always had the smell of liquor on his breath. So one evening I screamed at him that if he continued in his selfish ways he would not make a responsible father. Well it set off a terrible quarrel which then turned into a physical struggle. He raised his hand at me and I don't really remember much after that, except I awoke in the hospice and was told that I had lost the child.'

She looked down at her stomach and gently rested her hand on the space her baby might have grown within.

I shook my head remorsefully. 'I am so very sorry to hear this. It is such a terrible, terrible shame.'

'Yes it is, but it was nobody's fault dear Annie but my own. We were both young, foolish and equally strong-willed. It was whilst I was in recovery from my loss that Miss Leah Cunningham appeared in the doorway. At first I thought it was just some drug-induced vision I had acquired of her, but no... there she stood as clearly as I see you now. She came to see me after all the times I had tested her patience and said terribly mean things to her.

'She entered my room and sat beside me on the bed looking visibly shocked, though I could not blame her for it. We had not been the closest companions at the orphanage, but there was a certain empathy or understanding between us that remained unspoken.

'I remember how she glanced at my wedding finger. I suppose she realised then that I was not yet married to Jack, but I told her that I fully intended to marry him. My love for him blurred my senses. Despite his terrible treatment of me, the last thing I wished to do was return home to my parents.'

'And so did you marry him afterwards?' I asked.

She looked down at her lap in silence.

'Oh Miss Wakefield, say nothing more, clearly I can see it distresses you to speak of it.'

I could have persisted but the distress on her face was evident. I fingered the second note inside my purse but did not show it to her. I parted my lips to enquire about its meaning then closed them again. It did not feel an appropriate time.

'I really should depart now,' I said, standing to my feet. She nodded and escorted me to the door. I could see that the memories I had stirred had upset her.

'Please do not dwell upon the past any further Miss Wakefield. I shall visit again as soon as I am able to,' I promised.

I was anxious on my journey back and wished to learn more about Leah. I did not return home but headed straight back to the orphanage hoping that something new might be revealed.

I alighted from the carriage just a short distance from the entrance. I noticed a stillness in the air and a lack of birdsong in the trees. It was early afternoon yet darker than normal, and the wind stirred the leaves in every direction. It looked much like the beginning of another storm, or perhaps the angry stirrings of the same one which had awoken me the previous night.

I was greeted by the same elderly lady, whom I could not name, and without a word she led me straight into the main office.

The professional manner in which Miss De Bours received me made me admire her no-nonsense approach. I found it a sign of a well-to-do background and good breeding. This was a woman with a great degree of hardiness and seemingly confident in her role.

'A pleasure to see you once again, Miss Reinhart, what can I do for you?'

I took a seat opposite her, wondering if she had attached a slight note of sarcasm to her voice.

'I have some questions to ask, if I may.'

She nodded. 'I presume it is about your sister again?'

'Well yes actually. I do not feel that I am any closer to discovering what happened to her.'

She stared at me blankly.

'Miss Reinhart, I understand your desire to learn more about your sister, but I can only say that there simply isn't much to be offered aside from what we already have. My aim was to write a report on your sister, however, time was not favourable, and I cannot even be certain that I would find anything more than you already know.

'The mountain of archived records in the basement has suffered much damage due to damp and years of general disintegration, as unfortunately there was never a great pressing requirement to properly preserve it. Additionally, it would take many days, or even weeks, to pour through each document,'

I looked down at my lap with obvious signs of disappointment showing on my face.

Her voice softened and a tangle of lines formed on her brow.

'Miss Reinhart, it is not really our policy to part with confidential documents, but given that the subject is deceased many years, Mrs Stradlin did not object to passing you the paperwork. Was this not sufficient?'

'It does not contain much information at all.' I replied boldly. 'Did either of my parents ever enquire about my sister? Did they visit her or check on her welfare?'

She glared at me, somewhat irritated by my forward approach.

'There are no enquiries received upon the children once they enter the orphanage, and in many cases the children are either left abandoned or the parents quite often presumed dead.'

'No enquiries ever, you say?'

'No. Not ever. It is a last port of call for most of the children. We try to protect them. They begin a new life. Often there is no need too look back upon their past. Sadly, the world does not exist for the children outside these walls until they reach an age where they can be self-sufficient. It is better for them that they do not dredge up any difficult memories of their past.'

We sat silently for a moment as I digested these facts. An uneasy feeling of sadness floated between us, one that contained the essence of a million impenetrable hard truths and miseries to which I would likely never become aware.

When I finally spoke I noticed that the remaining light from the window had diminished almost entirely leaving a depressive atmosphere within the room.

'It seems so very sad to me, that children can be so unloved, Miss De Bours.'

She lowered her eyes and lit a desk lamp, sighing wearily as she did so. 'As I have confirmed to you before, the orphanage had received a Miss Primrose Amelia… '

'We called her Pixie,' I interjected. 'And I loved her dearly and not a day has passed that I have not thought about her. I was scolded for speaking of her when she left and I do not recall my parents ever visiting this place, not even when she passed away.'

She stared at me, puzzled by my words. 'Have your parents never once explained to you why they might have acted in such a way Miss Reinhart? You know it is a terrible shock that the child became mute and incapacitated. Perhaps they simply could not live with those facts?'

'Pixie survived,' I said coldly. 'She had been discarded by my parents and there was nothing I could do to prevent it. My mother had always suffered from a nervous mania, but to do this? Abandon her here? It does not seem right at all. I was contacted by Miss Wakefield and I have visited her, which has at least paved the way for some new contact.'

Her eyes widened with surprise.

'Miss Jeannie Wakefield?'

'Yes,' I confirmed. 'The same lady who resided here alongside my sister all those years ago.'

'And was she able to shed more light on the matter?'

I sighed deeply. 'Her own story is a tragic one. It seems she herself suffered greatly. I find it hard to question her too deeply, stirring up certain memories obviously upsets her, and in turn, she seems to find it difficult. Miss Wakefield did not have much association with my sister but she was close to somebody who was.'

'Who?'

'Miss Leah Cunningham. A girl aged just fourteen. I know very little about her. Does Leah have any family alive to speak of?'

She thought for a moment.

'Now you mention it I have heard of the name. The best I can do is look up some information, if we possess any that is. Would that be agreeable to you?'

'Yes, it would be most kind if you could look. If there is any living relative that you find, I would be most grateful to hear about it.'

'I will do my best.'

'Oh, I also have this,' I said retrieving the note from my purse, having almost forgotten about it.

I spoke to her this morning. Sister reported her as unresponsive in the aftermath. I fathom that she was not upset at our decision. She will be sent to the alternative place of residence in two days.

Mrs Matilda Featherstone.

Institutional Secretary

Miss De Bours read it carefully.

'Well, I have no idea who this note refers to Miss Reinhart. It does seem very odd indeed.'

A clock in the hallway loudly struck the hour of six.

'Ah...' she exclaimed. 'I must report back to my duties now. I apologise. Have you transport?'

'Yes, my carriage awaits outside.'

'Very good, sorry to cut you short. I will look up what I can regarding Miss Cunningham. If there is anything I find I shall pass it on to you.'

I left the orphanage to return home with feelings of disappointment as well as a renewed sense of hope.

Sixteen

Leah

The wooden blocks lay on the floor in an untidy pile. She reached forward to select one, turning it this way and that, taking time to appreciate the texture and size.

'Very good, hand it to me,' I encouraged her, and she did as I asked. I gave a little clap of approval.

We were sitting on the floor together in one of the smaller rooms in the orphanage that had an impressively large window which overlooked the tumbling hills beyond. Pixie was trying new activities that I had invented, where I would ask her to hand me a certain item and encourage her to show some interest in it.

But we were not alone.

Mrs Featherstone and Sister Ernestine quietly sat nearby and watched us intensely.

Nonetheless, Pixie was in a playful mood and I was very pleased with her behaviour. One of the bricks scattered away and she squealed with excitement, pointed at it then looked directly at me begging me to retrieve it. I did so and handed it back to her where she began to pile them again one by one on top of each other.

I looked at Sister Ernestine's face which showed no real sign of emotion, though Mrs Featherstone, I thought, appeared slightly dewy-eyed.

After some time had passed they stood to their feet and removed the chairs, placing them back against the wall.

'Thank you Miss Leah, you may continue.'

Once they'd left the room I closed my eyes and sighed with relief.

I had not expected the impromptu inspection and worried that she might behave hysterically. But I need not have been concerned as she paid little attention to her audience and continued to interact with me as she always did. I deeply hoped that they would be, if not impressed, at least satisfied with her progress as much as I was.

She was a girl damaged by fate, and I knew that I had gained enough trust from her by now that she was able to remain calm in my presence despite the onlookers in the room.

As the days passed I grew more fond of her. I felt a stab of pain at the thought that I might be removed from her care. These thoughts did little to dispel the fear I carried with me, but I knew it would be futile to brood over circumstances where I had little control, even where Miss Jeannie was concerned.

I had not forgotten my visit to her three weeks ago which still left me feeling sad and hopeless. She would be married now, and surely regretting her decision with every passing moment. It angered me that I had been unable to stop her from making such a foolish decision, and in equal measure, guilt lay upon me that I had interfered.

I pulled out the crumpled paper from my pocket.

I am so sorry Miss Leah. I did not wish to upset you. But I must marry him.

J

I had wanted to discard it the moment it was delivered to me, but I found I could not. Maybe it was the only link I would have to Jeannie ever again. I was surprised by the fact that she had, for once, apologised to me.

Pixie was beginning to tire of her activities. She placed her head on my lap and began to suck her thumb.

'Brave little girl,' I told her as I stroked her hair gently. I cradled her in my arms for a while and watched the droplets of rain tap against the window. A heavy cloud spread across the sky and darkened the whole room.

I heard the voices of other children talking and playing in a room beside ours and felt sad that Pixie could not run freely and have the pleasure of interacting with any of them. Sister strongly forbade it.

Would she always be alone? I wondered.

I bundled her up in my arms, strapped her to her chair and wheeled her to her room. Once I had settled her there I resumed the rest of my duties until later that evening Mrs Featherstone summoned me once again to her office.

'I am sorry for our intrusion this morning Leah, though I had informed you we would carry out an assessment on her progress. How do you feel Pixie is faring?'

I cleared my throat. 'I think you can see Madam, that she is doing very well. I know she is confident in my presence and trusts very few others.'

'Hmm yes,' she replied, tapping her chin with a finger.

'It is all well and good that she trusts you, however, Sister has raised some concerns. She feels that your attachment to her and vice versa could be detrimental.'

'Detrimental? In what way?' I stammered, my heart beating fast.

'Well, should something happen to you Miss Leah, and heaven's above we all pray to the contrary, would the child be adversely affected? Does such personal attention benefit her in the long run? We have many children here and our carers are already stretched to their capacity.'

'But she is improving, and she trusts me, is that not truly a positive thing?' I cut in, my tone defensive.

'Yes... yes, I do see that she is coming out of her shell and I see that she is content in your presence. I just hope that neither of you will suffer in time to come.'

Suffer in time to come....

What did she mean by that?

She turned and busied herself with collecting up a scattered pile of papers on her desk and placing them inside a drawer as she spoke.

'All of the abandoned children here, as we have discussed before, must learn how to cope in the world in which we live. There will come a time where many will seek a new life outside, that is if they survive these harsh conditions. As you know we do our best to raise them with the resources we have and through generous charitable assistance.

She closed the drawer roughly and faced me directly. In her eyes I saw a hidden sadness.

'But we are *not* their parents, Leah, we can never be parents to these children and we simply do not have the capacity to provide individual care.'

'Mrs Featherstone,' I pleaded. 'I have been performing every duty you have allocated to me. I scrub, clean, bathe the babies, wash the latrines, scrub the hearths, the blackened pots and pans. I do whatever it is that Sister requires of me, and still I manage to do this whilst attending to Pixie. I beg you. Please do not alter my status.'

Her eyes looked down at my hands which were trembling in my lap. I could tell that she was contemplating my words.

'You must calm yourself Leah. I had no intention of removing you from her care. I only wish to highlight the reality of the situation. Should more children be placed with us we will need to re-assess the situation. Be prepared for anything... and nothing. We are quite stretched as it is and I must be careful who we take on for these responsible positions.'

I recalled Pixie's father. Perhaps he had said something after our unexpected meeting outside her room. Perhaps he did not approve of me for some reason. Or could it be Sister? Had she said something after the inspection in an attempt to thwart my role?

'Why did Pixie's father pay her a visit?' I asked, surprised that I had uttered the words aloud.

She came towards me, gently took my hand and led me to the door, her serious expression changing into one of kindness again.

'We do not discuss the families or outside connections of any of the orphans here. I am sorry but you must go back to your duties now, I have a great amount of work to do. You are a well-behaved girl and you have done nothing untoward so do not let our little talk upset you so.'

I nodded and left her office. It was impossible not to feel unsettled as I returned to my duties. Later that afternoon I used my solitary time to sit behind the building under the lengthening shadows of a bushy tree. I was glad of the peace since I had earlier been assisting Mrs O'Flaherty with teaching some of the children how to tie their shoe laces which had ended in fits of laughter. Mrs O'Flaherty tried to remain serious but even she eventually succumbed to their infectious laughter. She had much less patience than I though, and even as my spirits were lifted by the fact that I had achieved so much with Pixie, I now felt utterly despondent.

I stared glumly ahead. The grass was wet and muddy. A small bird flew down and landed beside me, chirping as if to communicate a message, then flew away. My thoughts became muddled. I could only conclude that Mrs Featherstone was becoming disillusioned with my service because of Sister, who quite clearly showed her disapproval of my relationship with Pixie.

I looked up at the brooding sky and guessed that it would be about time I provided Pixie with some nourishment.

Just as I was about to rise, I heard a twig snap on the ground behind me. I turned around to see Miss Jeannie standing there in a thick grey woollen coat and a wide-brimmed hat pulled low over her face.

'JEANNIE!'

My voice rose in an excited pitch. 'What are you doing here?'

She lifted her chin and beamed at me. 'Isn't it obvious? I am back!'

She placed herself beside me and took hold of my hand. I could not help but laugh as her face lit up with a familiar playful grin.

'You could not be rid of me that easily Miss Leah. I do hope my bed is still available? And you know something? You were right. It would have been a terrible mistake to marry Jack.'

Seventeen

Annie

'I know that it was strange of me to call you so suddenly but I discovered something. Information which I think you would be interested in learning and could lead to further revelations regarding your sister.'

I braced myself for the worst and tried to sit as comfortably as I could, having spent the whole journey to the orphanage worrying about the information Miss De Bours wished to part. It was impossible to tell by the tone of her voice whether I would be pleasantly surprised or otherwise.

When I entered the familiar office I found her expression relaxed and free from any tell-tale sign of anxiety, something which I recognised all too well in my mother. She sat across from me with her hair loosely pinned at the nape of her neck, appearing much more at ease than during our last encounter, where I supposed she possibly felt irritated by my unannounced appearance, followed by my persistent line of questioning.

'There is every good chance you may find out more about Miss Leah Cunningham herself,' she continued.

'I have looked through some of the older records and I was able to source a document which linked Leah to a lady named Mrs Emily Staves. It appears that Emily is the eldest daughter of a Mr Ronald Staves, a military officer who had suffered from a heart condition. Miss Cunningham cared for him at St Margaret's Home for the Elderly in Eastbourne Street.'

She glanced up to see my reaction but I only stared at her open-mouthed and with great anticipation.

'Miss Cunningham left the orphanage in the winter of 1882, just a few days after the sad passing of your sister. It seems possible that this position was found for her in the aftermath of the event. Though I am afraid this is all information we possess. How or why she left, I can locate no records I am afraid. I think you might have more luck if you contact Miss Staves yourself, the details of which I can pass on to you.'

My gratitude unfolded with the wide smile I offered to her.

'This is wonderful news. I thank you from the bottom of my heart, but as there is no detail on record as to why Leah left the orphanage, perhaps she felt too upset to remain here after my sister's death. Either that or her services were no longer required, perhaps.'

Miss De Bours contemplated my words.

'Hmm. Well that would explain the note which you showed to me. I agree, there were always countless orphans brought into this home and they would have used every pair of hands they could, so why she left does seem a bit of a mystery. I do hope Miss Staves can shed further light on the matter. Sorry I could not be any more helpful.'

'Oh you have helped much more than I expected and I apologise for troubling you, and also for turning up unannounced on my previous visit.'

She smiled. 'You are welcome Miss Reinhart, yes we do sometimes have busier days than others and I do understand your need to find out about your sister. Well, if you do not mind I will see you to your carriage.'

We left the office together. I remembered that I was to meet Matthew in fifty minutes at The Berney Arms, some two miles away.

'And how is your Mother keeping?' Miss De Bours asked as we exited the building.

'I am afraid her health varies somewhat day by day. She has a nervous disposition which is terribly taxing on her.'

She nodded sympathetically.

'Well, goodbye Miss Reinhart. Good luck on your search.'

She waved me away as I settled into my seat. I realised that weeks had flown past again since my last visit to Mother, something which I was subconsciously aware of but all too easily had overlooked.

Poor Bessie had contacted me many times to report on her health. Often she informed me that Mother wished not to be disturbed and I often wondered if this was truly the case, or just an excuse to deter me from visiting, for I believed that even Bessie herself was cautious to invite me. By now she was familiar with our strained conversation and contemptuous relationship.

I decided that I would see Matthew then possibly pay Mother a visit if Bessie revealed that she was in good form.

I tucked the piece of paper with Miss Staves's details into my purse. I had no idea what the lady might reveal regarding Leah or Pixie but I was very keen to meet with her, so much so that I felt more excitement locked in those thoughts than in the knowledge that I was on my way to see my fiancée.

This inner revelation unsettled me slightly for it is not as if I could deny my love for Matthew. I could not say exactly how I felt, but it just seemed more like my ardent affection for him had begun to wane recently, my mind being occupied elsewhere.

As we made our way to the west of the city, I attempted to push the troublesome feelings of doubt away before they began to fester in my heart.

Eighteen

Leah

The cheery bells of Christmas rang every day of the week leading up to the festive holiday and there was a continuous pulse of near feverish excitement leading right up to the day. All the children from the oldest to the youngest had learned festive songs which had been taught to them by the orphanage staff.

The sky looked clear and bright as each child stood lined up one crisp morning outside the orphanage to perform to the local dignitaries, including the village Mayor and his wife.

The orphans had been washed and scrubbed scrupulously the previous night in order to kill any lingering fleas or insects they might have been carrying. The stench of carbolic soap still lingered inside many rooms of the building, though their scrubbed faces and coarsely brushed hair somehow saddened me, for I knew that it was intended only for the benefit of the audience they were made to perform to.

I stood to one side of the grounds beside a large potted shrub. Pixie sat quietly in her chair. She had allowed me to wash her more thoroughly the previous evening without waving her arms and wailing at my attempts to lather her hair. Now she seemed only too content to watch the scene.

The strange girl in the chair, as she had been dubbed by other children, was usually completely ignored. A sad fact for Pixie but perhaps a blessing all the same, since she was far too anxious and unequipped to deal with the varying ways in which the children communicated with each other.

At the end of the performances the Mayor and his wife came over to greet us. I saw that she was a petite woman who wore very high shoes and a large brimmed hat from which she peered at us with a painted smile. I curtseyed as she leaned forward to ask Pixie her name.

'She does not speak,' I told her as politely as I could.

The mayor's wife nodded, stepped back, then looked away as though there were little point in further effort being made with an orphan who could not communicate.

I was glad. Pixie did not trust strangers.

'Look what a marvellous little chair she has,' said the Mayor to his wife who was now distracted and peering across the grounds to see which person she might approach next.

'Who is the manufacturer of this contraption?' he asked me, puffing at a long cigar.

'I do not know, Sir,' I replied honestly. 'I heard it may be the medical person himself who took her into his care.'

'Well it's bloody marvellous,' he responded. He poked at the rickety wheels attached to the wooden legs, oblivious to the tiny girl who began to shrink away with fear inside it.

I placed a comforting hand on her shoulder as she clutched her doll tightly, crossing my fingers behind my back and praying that the

Mayor and his wife would leave before Pixie erupted into a hysterical fit.

Fortunately, Mrs Featherstone called over to the Mayor and he took three large puffs of his pipe, clasped his wife's arm somewhat roughly and strode away leaving a thick cloud of black smoke in his wake.

I was relieved that the public event had finally come to an end.

The following day the children enjoyed the task of creating small gifts for each member of staff, mainly designed using the scattered leaves and other small items they had picked from the gardens. The orphanage rooms were scattered with twigs, leaves and acorns for many days, which we all had to pitch in together and brush away.

Donations from various societies and churches poured in throughout the month of December, including ribbons, pretty scented soaps, string, buttons, pins, fabric and other useful knick-knacks the orphans could use to create gifts and decorations.

A large tree was erected in the main hall decorated with colourful paper lanterns, wreaths and dried fruits wrapped into bundles and set on the mantelpiece of each room. They had been sent from the village. On Christmas Eve, the children placed their pretty gifts wrapped in pieces of rough fabric and paper beneath the tree.

A Mass was performed in the chapel to give thanks for all that we were fortunate to possess. I held on to Pixie's hand at the back as we sang loudly and a few children performed short theatrical plays in the hall that same afternoon.

Pixie sucked on her thumb and appeared amused by a boy dressed as a court jester who cart-wheeled along the hall wearing ridiculous shoes made of scrap bits of paper and bells tied to the end with string. He reminded me of our visit to the circus.

When the evening came to a close the children were sent to sleep in their dormitories. I was filled with gratitude in the comfort and safety I felt at the orphanage. It also occurred to me that I ought to try and source a small gift or perhaps take a trip to the village to see if I could obtain something for Mrs Featherstone, Sister Ernestine and Miss Jeannie.

On Christmas morning, when I had fully expected to resume my duties as normal, Miss Jeannie came rushing in the room to speak with me as I leaned over a bucket to begin scrubbing a huge pile of soiled napkins.

'Come quickly, Miss Leah, oh I don't know how to begin to tell you,'

'What is it?' I asked nervously.

'Follow me downstairs, but we must not be seen.'

I dropped the napkin from my hand and did as she asked, treading down the staircase fearing what I was about to witness. When we reached the bottom Jeannie pulled me to one side where we cowered beneath the staircase peering inside the window of Mrs Featherstone's office. And there sat my father with a woman I did not recognise for I had never before seen her in my life. She looked stern and wore an oversized coat. She also wore a large floppy blue hat that partly obscured her face. I saw that she was talking animatedly whilst my father appeared red-faced beside her, staring mournfully at his shoes.

We pressed our ears as hard as we could to the door in an effort to hear the conversation inside.

'She has no desire to leave,' I could hear Mrs Featherstone saying. 'She is a blessing to us, and many of the children look up to her so you can see how your demands would affect not only your daughter, but the children who are so very fond of her.'

I looked at Jeannie whose eyes were wide with curiosity.

'Do you know this woman?' she asked me.

'No, but I can guess. It must be Elsie, the lady my father began to live with not long after my mother passed away.'

'She looks like the bad sort to me Miss Leah, what do you think they both want?'

I sighed. 'Do you remember the last time he was here? Begging for compensation for my services and Mrs Featherstone delivered him a sharp talking to.'

She pressed her ear harder to the glass which was partially obscured by a netted curtain.

'I do remember, and it looks like he is back to try again and this time with his mistress.'

'Oh what will I do?' I panicked, grabbing a hold of her hand.

She looked at me directly, thinking as she did with great deliberation. 'I do not know what you should do but I am certain that Mrs Featherstone will find some way to be rid of them. We must trust in her knowledge and good judgement.'

I agreed but could not stop my hands from trembling. If only I was as strong as Miss Jeannie and could face my troubles without feeling so helpless.

The woman inside the office did not possess an honest face, she looked every bit as sly as I had imagined her to be, and she spoke loudly and rudely, digging her elbow into my father's side so that he should back up whatever it was she was saying.

If they were truly here to beg for money again, I do not know how Mrs Featherstone would find another excuse to send them packing. I was still a minor, at an age where my father still had full guardianship of me. If he wished to remove me from this orphanage he was entitled to do so and there was not a single thing Mrs Featherstone, I, or Miss Jeannie could do about it.

I watched the scene before me, feeling my legs weaken with every passing moment. Mrs Featherstone appeared defeated. Her cheeks blazed red with what could only be described as unwarranted harassment. Suddenly she rose to her feet as the meeting seemed to come to an end.

Jeannie and I jumped out of view and hid beneath the staircase as they emerged from the office.

'And there won't be any need for me to return will there? I'm sure you will do as we have asked,' said Elsie.

Mrs Featherstone nodded, and I felt my heart sink to the very pit of my stomach.

The couple walked on ahead and disappeared around a corner and we waited until their footsteps could no longer be heard.

Mrs Featherstone approached us.

'Miss Jeannie and Miss Leah you can emerge from your hiding place now.'

She showed great concern on her face. I felt sorry for the kind lady who I felt did not deserve such treatment.

Jeannie and I stood with our heads bowed low.

'What have I said before about eavesdropping?' Especially you Miss Wakefield. I have told you more than once not to dally about outside doors or eavesdrop upon a person's private conversation.'

We apologised in unison and she placed a hand on my shoulder.

'I must talk to you alone. Miss Jeannie please resume your duties.'

'Yes Madam,' she replied, glancing at me with concern in her eyes before walking away.

We entered the office.

'It is not good news Miss Leah, but I must tell you that I hope you will not assume that I have any part to play in this new decision.'

'Which decision?' I mumbled, feeling tears well up in my eyes.

'Your father and his mistress are to take you away to live with them. They obviously feel that they require you to help them earn a living.' She looked remorseful as she spoke and I broke down into loud sobs.

'Oh Mrs Featherstone, how can we stop them. I do not want to leave, please, is there nothing you can do to help?'

'I have tried my very best. There is nothing that I can do.'

She handed me a handkerchief to wipe my tears.

'How long have I left?' I asked.

'Three days.'

'Is that all?'

'Yes child,' she said, moving closer to me. 'Now please Miss Leah, lift your eyes to the world and be brave. I know this change will be hard for you but you are a resourceful young woman and you must face life's trials and tribulations with courage.'

'But what about Pixie?' I asked.

'Pixie will be cared for and you may return to visit her. Take some time for yourself now. I will tell sister that you will resume your duties later this afternoon.'

I nodded, stood up and thanked her before leaving, shutting the door behind me gently. I found that I could not return to Pixie that afternoon at all. The news of my impending departure revealed new layers of sadness within me. How would I even tell her? I could not look her in the eye. She would never understand or forgive me.

I despised my father in that moment, that he cared so little about my own feelings and would allow his mistress to take possession of his good nature. If my mother were still alive she would never have allowed such foul treatment of me.

Locking the door to my room I threw myself onto the bed and cried from the deepest part of my soul. Once the tears ran dry I began to write in the diary in unintelligible scribbles, my tears smudging the ink across the page.

Some words I recorded in the tiniest letters I could manage where only I might be able to decipher them.

Again and again I wrote words backwards that only I could read. Words intended to plan my escape from Father and his mistress Elsie.

Nineteen

Annie

'Annie, over here!'

I caught sight of Matthew waving from our usual seating area at the corner of the dining establishment with a smile that spread from ear to ear. He wore the same light grey tailored travelling suit and hat that I was accustomed to seeing. My heart sank at the indifference I felt upon viewing him.

'Hello darling,' I called, approaching the table with as decent a smile as I could muster.

We embraced and I caught a whiff of his familiar woody scent.

'Good journey?'

'Pleasant enough, frightfully cold on the train however. Are we having supper?'

'Yes, why not,' I replied, picking up the menu.

We were to spend the weekend together before he returned to Cornwall. During his visits we often dined out, leaving poor Mrs Bryne without cooking duties for many an evening.

Dependable, hard-working Matthew was a good catch, though Mother would always pick him apart and wheedle out his few flaws, placing them under a microscope and turning them into gigantic obstacles. She could not understand how he allowed me to keep hold of my single status title, as if I might fare better if he were a dictator of some sort. She viewed him as weak and overly tolerant.

It made me wonder, as I watched him scanning the menu, if it was actually Mother who had slowly weaved a web of doubt within our relationship.

'Looking radiant as ever Annie,' he said, taking my hand and kissing it affectionately. 'Are we having the same?'

'Hmm?'

He tipped my chin towards him. 'Annie, are we having the same as usual, veal and potato dauphinoise?'

'Oh yes, of course, if you like,' I replied.

He put the menu down.

'What is it Annie, is everything all right?'

'Yes of course it is,' I replied as a waiter arrived to fill our glasses with a dark coloured wine.'

'And how is your mother, or should I not ask?' He lifted his glass to his lips and took a long sip.

'Oh,' I rolled my eyes. 'Where does one begin? She is as difficult as ever.'

'Have you visited her recently?'

'Not for a few weeks,' I said, skimming the menu vacantly.

The waiter arrived and took our order. It was the same one as always. I looked at Matthew hoping to see something new about him, but there was nothing new at all to remark upon. His chin was cleanly shaven and his hair brushed into the same neat side parting.

'You look well,' I managed to say.

He smiled and leaned closer to me, touching my forearm affectionately.

I stiffened.

'Matthew, please, we are surrounded by diners.'

'Oh humbug, who cares about them, Annie.'

'I do,' I replied testily.

He leaned back and viewed me with a serious expression.

'Something is up Annie, come on tell me, what is it?'

I scratched at the lobe of my ear, a habit which revealed my inner anxiety. I sighed, and decided then to confess.

'I finally visited that children's orphanage,' I said, avoiding his eyes.

There was a moment of silence.

'Oh, right, the one in Greenwich you mean?'

'Yes, you know, the one Pixie was sent to after the…'

'Yes, yes after that terrible accident, yes I know about that.'

Our starter of quail egg and French toast arrived. He split the yolk with a fork.

'I went there to seek information, you know, to see if they could tell me what her life was like.'

He chewed on his food slowly.

'Annie you know my viewpoint on this. We have had this conversation many times, but well, if you persist in looking into the past, who am I to stop you?'

I bit my tongue before responding and we ate silently for a while, the tension between us palpable. I could feel him thinking about what he should say as opposed to what he felt it was necessary to say.

'I am sorry. Tell me what you discovered there, if anything at all,' he piped up after a while.

A waiter re-filled our glasses.

'Well, I discovered that she is buried there at the orphanage. I suspected it, anyway. Though it was a rather poor excuse for a grave. I am disappointed.'

He nodded. 'I am sorry.'

'Don't be.'

'What else did you discover?'

'Not much. Well, you know she didn't live for very long and they found that recorded entry about her choking.'

'Yes, it is extremely sad,' he agreed. 'But it was a quarter of a century ago Annie. Things are much changed and very different now.'

'And I met a lady who once worked there,' I continued, 'she was kind and welcoming, though I must have stirred up some bitter memories. I felt extremely awkward about it.'

He took my hand gently in his. 'Your mother won't approve, you know that.'

'I know. She is stubborn on the matter, but it is not for her peace of mind Matthew, it is for mine.'

'Are you sure? Are you sure that it's just for you?'

He threw up his hands in frustration. 'Do you really want to confront your mother now?'

My face reddened. 'Matthew, I don't wish to confront my mother. I am making enquiries for myself,' I said flatly, revealing only a part-truth.

The second course arrived and I stared at my plate feeling an urge to pick it up and throw it across the restaurant.

'Annie, I won't continue to object, I just hope you know what you are doing. I don't think your Mother has even gotten over the loss of Gerald.'

'My Father hasn't anything to do with this.' I snapped.

'You said she talks of him as if he were still alive.'

'She does, but it has nothing to do with my sister.' I poked a fork at the veal and felt my appetite dissolve.

'You do tend to upset her Annie, what with this huge grudge of yours.'

I stared at him open-mouthed. 'Grudge? What huge grudge? And I suppose you think it is acceptable for my Mother to upset *me*?'

'Of course not. But she is mentally incapacitated.'

He lowered his voice.

'Look I know you feel a need to dredge up the past, but your Mother obviously doesn't. Can't you just accept that?'

I looked away, tears forming in my eyes. How dare he cause me to become emotional in a public setting. I placed my fork down and leaned away from him.

'Look, let's not start the weekend together quarrelling. Please?' He took hold of my arm. 'Tell me about your art students. Is young Alfie still the prodigious worldly artist you predicted?'

His attempt to change the subject and placate my mood almost made me want to scream hysterically, and I realised that a visit to my mother following our lunch date would now be absolutely out of the question.

'Yes,' I said coldly, picking up my fork again and taking a small bite of my meal which had now turned stone cold.

'Good,' he said and held up his glass.

'No. Look. I'm sorry. I want to leave,' I told him standing to my feet. 'Let's go home.'

'Are you all right,' he asked, concerned.

'Yes. Yes, I just need to retire to bed. It's been a long day and I fear this whole conversation has brought on a migraine.'

Twenty

Leah

I confirm this as being my last recorded entry at the Greenwich Orphanage Institution.

I am forced to leave today. I cannot bring myself to visit her room, look at her face, or tell her that I will not be returning here again. I feel that in some way I have failed her. When I think of all the promises I made to her, promises which she must have believed deeply in her heart, it pains me to think that I have let her down against my own will.

But somehow, I must keep my courage and not lose faith. If I were to become ill through sadness and pity how will I ever return to her? She may weep for me but I will shed more tears for her. Oh Pixie, my sweet child.

I can find no forgiveness in my heart for my

father. His cruel and incalculable actions have erased any affection I might have once felt for him. Goodness knows what I am about to face. I pray the Lord carry me in his arms with his own strength as I face a new and uncertain future.

If there were any way I could change...

'Are you ready?' Sister Ernestine called.

I was surprised to see an expression of sadness on her face as she stood at the door of my room.

'Yes, I am,' I confirmed, closing the diary and slipping it into my case. I swallowed hard and wiped a tear from my eye.

Miss Jeannie walked in, linked her arm tightly in mine and picked up the case which was packed with my few possessions.

'You must visit us soon. Promise me that we will not lose contact.'

I nodded and together we descended the winding staircase and headed towards the entrance of the building where the horse and carriage awaited. I stepped outside and inhaled the familiar musty scent of damp earth. A few blurry stars blinked in the rose coloured sky.

Some members of staff and children were gathered at the entrance to wish me well on my journey. There was no sign of Pixie however, and I raised my chin and tried hard not to weep again. I had been unable to visit her after hearing the news of my departure. I despised my own weakness. I did not find the courage to face her and tell her that I would be leaving permanently, fearful that I would never ever see her again. She would detest me, the trust she had built crumbling in an instant. More than anything, I hoped that Sister Ernestine would not treat her roughly or neglect her.

'Goodbye,' I said, my voice cracking as I descended the few steps.

I mounted the carriage then Mrs Featherstone closed the door and touched my hand gently.

'Thank you for all you have done for us here Miss Leah. I do hope you will stay well and find happiness.'

I gave a thankful nod and she waved the driver on. I could not look back at the faces I had become so dearly fond of, so instead I chose to stare silently at the trees and twisting paths unfolding as we journeyed towards my new home a good distance away from the orphanage.

A new chapter in my life was about to begin where Pixie played no part. One day, when I found it possible to return here I would tell her that I had not willingly abandoned her and played no part in the cruel decision.

Whether she would understand or not I had no idea, but I decided that I would tell her all the truths that lay inside my heart.

Twenty-One

Annie

I picked up the telephone handset and asked the operator to pass me through. She connected me to Miss Staves line.

'Is that Miss Staves? Hello there?'

'Yes, good day...' came a woman's voice sounding a fair distance away.

'Ah hello, I am Annie Reinhart...'

'What... who... sorry? I can barely hear, please speak up, I'm afraid I am not too acquainted with this dreadful machinery.'

'Hello my name is Annie Reinhart. Do you have a free moment to speak?' I said loudly.

There was an awkward silence for a few seconds and further crackling.

'Oh yes, hello Miss Reinhart how may I help you?'

'I acquired your contact details from the children's Orphanage in Greenwich. I am searching for information on a Miss Leah Cunningham. Would you happen to have heard of this young lady who once worked there?'

There was a pause.

'Why yes, yes I do. I have heard of her, but what is the purpose of your enquiry may I ask?'

'Well she was a carer to my late twin sister, many years ago I might add, and I was merely hoping to fill in the gaps. Would it be possible to meet with you?'

'Of course though I am afraid I will be away for a fortnight the day after tomorrow, so if you are free I could possibly spare an hour tomorrow afternoon? Where do you reside?'

'Oh...' I said, pausing.

I knew that Matthew would be upset if I interrupted our weekend plans, especially when he was due to leave on Monday. But if I did not agree to meet her now I would have to wait for two more weeks.

'Is that all right with you?' she asked again.

'Yes, yes I can make it, just inform me of an appropriate time and place. I live in Chelsea.'

'Excellent. Do you know the fabulous café at the corner of Margate Street called The Dime? I could meet you there, it is about halfway between us?'

I smiled into the telephone receiver. 'Perfect. That is just a thirty minute journey from where I am situated.'

'Excellent,' she replied. 'Is three o' clock acceptable to you?'

'Yes! Thank you. I shall be there. And thank you so much for your kindly response.'

'My pleasure Miss Reinhart. See you tomorrow then.'

I ended the call feeling elated. There would be more to find out about Leah, of that I was certain, and perhaps if I was truly lucky, Miss Staves had something the girl might have kept in her possession. Something that might have even been touched by my sister's own hand?

Oh the thought!

It lifted my spirits even though I knew I was being far too hopeful.

I walked to the hallway and saw Matthew's heavy case on the floor. My smile faded instantly. He had gone into the main town to purchase a newspaper. I would have to tell him about my date with Miss Staves when he returned and I began to fear that he would not be impressed.

I heard the key in the lock and almost jumped out of my skin. I hadn't expected him to return quite so soon.

'I am back my dearest,' he called out cheerfully.

I hurried to the table, donned my apron and picked up a brush from the wooden box. I then dipped it into a small pot and began to spread ochre yellow across a scenic river painting set on its easel; a new painting that I had been working on.

'Ah, there you are! Hmm, have you not finished that one yet?' he said glancing over at me as he removed his coat.

'Yes, it's coming along well, just a little slowly', I replied, trying to find the courage to tell him about my meeting.

'Matthew,' I began hesitantly as he threw his coat behind the chair and sat down to read his paper. 'Have you made a plan for us tomorrow afternoon? Only I would like to pay a quick visit to an acquaintance.'

'An acquaintance? What sort of an acquaintance?' he said flicking through the pages.

'Well she isn't really much of an acquaintance I suppose, she is connected to the orphanage.'

He turned to face me and slowly shook his head.

'Annie. I thought we had gone over this. When did you arrange to meet this person? We said we would spend the weekend together, alone, visiting the art gallery amongst other things.'

'Yes, I know! And we can! This is just a quick meeting Matthew. Can't you see how much this means to me?'

He frowned. 'You made no mention of this at all yesterday, why not?'

I let out long breath, feeling defeated by my own stupidity. To think I could outsmart him was senseless.

'Shall I just leave now Annie? Take the next train back to Cornwall?'

'No that is not what I meant Matthew, please,' I begged.

'When did you speak to this lady?' he persisted.

I rubbed my earlobe, an action which betrayed my inner anxiety.

'This morning, Matthew. She told me she would only be available tomorrow. I could not get another appointment with her for some time.'

'She is only available tomorrow? Right I see, and I suppose this is all to do with your long dead twin sister again isn't it?'

I inhaled a sharp breath. 'Matthew!'

'What Annie?' he said, now rising to his feet. His nostrils flared with anger. 'As far as I can tell you are more interested in persisting with this adventure than spending time with me! And what of our wedding plans? You have not mentioned them at all. The subject is always Pixie. Every visit I make you always bring her up! Heaven forbid, if she was at all able to be lifted from her tomb I suppose you would have her dine with us too!'

'Good God, Matthew!' My hands rose to my face. 'How could you even say such a terrible thing?'

The spiteful remark tore at my heart and I dropped the paint brush I was holding. It landed on the carpet leaving a splash of yellow.

'Now I can see why you were so keen for me to visit the store this morning, asking me to purchase a paper so that you could make your enquiries without my presence.'

He threw the newspaper down on the armchair, picked up his coat and strode to the door.

'Well my dear Annie whatever it is you hope to achieve I hope it is for your own benefit, please don't let me stand in your way.'

He walked outside and slammed the door shut behind him.

I felt a deep painful sob rise in my chest as I watched him through the window. He swung his arms as he walked and I promptly hated myself for driving him away.

At that moment the telephone rang and I jumped, hurrying across the room to answer the caller and knocking the easel so that the painting slid off the floor to unite with the brush. I howled loudly before picking up the receiver, my hand shaking as I placed it to my ear.

'Yes, yes, hello?' I said quietly trying to compose myself and hoping that the caller could not detect the tremor in my voice.

'Annie?' came a woman's faint voice.

'Yes?'

'It's Bessie here,'

'Oh. Good morning Bessie. Is everything all right?' I stammered.

'I am afraid it isn't Annie, I think you should come over right away.'

My heart lurched.

'Why? Is Mother all right, has something happened?'

There was a pause.

'I am very sorry to tell you this Annie, but your Mother has suffered a stroke.'

Twenty-Two

Leah

The first thing I noticed upon entering the room was the stench of over boiled vegetables. A large blackened pan on the range bubbled away loudly. My eyes absorbed the room as a whole and I could not help but gasp aloud.

Elsie Cairn's home was an unsightly cavern of chaos. A child's legs stuck out between the cushions of a worn armchair, soiled clothing lay scattered about in every direction, and when I glanced up I saw that the roof had a wide hole that had been patched up with rags. Everywhere my eyes came to rest seemed to be in total disarray.

In a chair beside the window sat Elsie with a wriggling toddler splayed across her lap. She seemed to be struggling to change the boy's clothing, whilst he chewed on a knuckle of bread.

She cast her eyes over me without showing any sign of interest.

'Come in then.' Her tone was flat. 'You might as well get settled in.'

I moved a few steps forward and set down my case near a vacant chair. 'Where is my father?' I asked.

She glanced over at the window. 'Out there doing his best to earn a crumb.'

I seated myself, unsure where to look or what to do, for it was by far worse than the orderly and disciplined structure I had been accustomed to at the orphanage. At the very least the staff there did their best to keep an appropriate level of hygiene, but it appeared that Elsie had very little concern in that regard.

Another child I had not noticed before crawled out from beneath a cupboard. He eyed me curiously. He must have been near Pixie's age.

I swallowed a lump in my throat.

'Yeah I got five of these nippers altogether,' began Elsie, 'hard work they are I tell ya, perhaps you can 'elp me get them turnips and spinach over there mashed up while I set the table.'

I did as she asked, moving aside a soiled napkin which had been left to deteriorate beside the cooking pot.

'Ain't had time to clear up the mess yet,' she said.

My heart swiftly sank at the thought of having to spend the rest of my days here. 'Where am I to sleep, do I have a room?'

She snorted loudly.

'A room? Just for you? Bleeding heck, is it Her Majesty's fancy palace that you've come away from?

'I'm sorry,' I replied, as I ladled soggy cabbage into a wooden bowl. 'I had shared quarters with another girl, but the orphanage is big and has plenty of room.'

'Yes I know. I've been in it once meself. It used to be an Abbey you know until all them monks died of some gawd-knows-what plague that happened hundreds of years ago.'

She slid the infant off her lap and placed him on the ground, handing him a tatty shoe lace to chew between his swollen gums.

'You'll be sleeping on the floor until we can get summit sorted, but don't despair, once you find work tomorrow we'll put summat aside for her Ladyship's new room.'

She gave a loud cackle, flashing discoloured teeth. I wished I could dissolve into the floor instantly.

'Is this the only room?' I asked sheepishly.

I hadn't expected anything fancy by any means but my parents and I were lucky enough to have three rooms when we had been better off. Things changed when Father frittered away all his earnings and my mother's savings, then consequently lost his position.

'Ain't no more room than what yer standing in right now my girl,' she responded. 'But yer old man and I will be sleeping on a mattress over there.' She pointed to a filthy curtain drawn in the corner that was pegged up with bits of string.

'Two of the bairns go in that cot and the other two lie on a blanket on the floor, but you get the privilege to choose where you want to sleep,' she laughed.

I felt suddenly ill and contemplated dropping the bowl of vegetables and running for the door, but it opened as my thought took hold and we both looked across to see my father walk in.

He was a shell of his former self. I lowered my eyes as he lifted his head to view me then looked away.

My heart ached for the loving father whom I had once looked up to with deep affection. A man who doted on me with responsibility and affection. I noticed that his eyes held a look of deep sorrow and he slumped into the armchair paying little attention to his surrounding, or to me as I mashed the vegetables. Under Elsie's instructions I dished out several servings on small chipped plates that still bore dried remnants of an earlier meal.

Nobody sat together at the table to consume their food. The children clambered on top of each other on to a rickety stool and picked at their plates messily. Father did not eat at all and Elsie took her plate beside the window. I forced myself to eat a few mouthfuls then returned to my chair in the corner of the room. I had only been sitting for a few moments when Elsie commanded that I help with another chore, and then another. It soon dawned on me that the reason for my presence was to become her unpaid skivvy maid, one she could never afford to employ but for whom she could spare a mouthful of stewed vegetables.

My resentment grew evident in my manner as I refused to interact with the grubby disobedient children or make conversation with the adults. Father spoke only to tell me that we would rise at dawn and I would seek work the following day.

I was taken aback. 'What work am I to seek?'

'Anything you can find my girl. We ain't got no uppity privileges in this area that would allow us to pick n' choose,' sneered Elsie.

I sat solemnly in the corner for the rest of the evening, bringing out the diary to read from time to time. Elsie sniggered at my attempt to hide my activity.

'Writing some fancy story are ya?' she jeered whilst pegging a few clothes onto a piece of string by the fireplace. 'Better be good then, it might make us all wealthy.'

I turned away from her sneers and prayed that I might survive under the same roof as the despicable woman and her ill mannered brood. When my eyes began to feel tired I settled myself on the floor with two ragged cushions and a thin blanket, curled up to face the wall so that I did not have to view the other occupants in the room.

I sobbed silently to myself, sorely missing Pixie and Miss Jeannie. If I had the courage I would have walked all the way back to the orphanage, but at what cost? Elsie would only make her way there again to demand that I return.

The young children sniffled loudly in their cot, and I heard the door open and close shut. When I looked up I saw a young boy enter. He looked only a year or two younger than I. He eyed me disdainfully then sneered and removed his cap, throwing it across the room. I did not expect him to snatch away the blanket which covered my body only partially, for I dared not even remove my outer clothing.

'What's this all about? Who gave her my blanket?'

'Shush' came Elsie's voice behind the curtain. 'To bed with ya Freddy, she'll be earning one of her own soon.'

He threw a grimace my way and moved over to the armchair, belched loudly and settled under his blanket without removing his grubby clothes.

I turned away and put both my hands over my face. There I sobbed for the rest of the night as silently as I could.

Twenty-Three

Annie

'She is asleep but please be gentle with her,' said Bessie as I entered the room.

Mother lay on her back in a room that was bathed in dim light. The curtains were drawn tightly. It was early afternoon but felt more like midnight.

'When did it happen?' I asked Bessie.

She sighed wearily.

'Just after dawn, we thought she'd had another of her crying fits but her eyes rolled back so I sent for the physician. He confirmed that she had suffered a stroke and that there isn't much we can do Annie, except make her comfortable when she awakens. How much it has affected her senses I cannot tell you.'

I nodded, bearing the weight of her words.

'I will leave you awhile,' she said closing the door gently.

I sat on the edge of the bed and took Mother's hand in mine. It felt cold despite the warmth in the room and I was surprised by the lightness of it. Her physical frailty now seemed to match her mental state, but she appeared peaceful and serene, floating in a place where her thoughts and memories could not trouble her.

She appeared not like a victim who had suffered a stroke, but a woman who had slipped out of her shell and gone to a more peaceful haven, for her breathing was calm. I stroked her hand, all my grudges towards her quickly dissolving.

She stirred.

'Water,' she muttered under her breath.

'Mother, it's me,' I whispered.

'Annie?'

'I am here.'

'What happened to me?'

'You fainted. It was a bad spell, nothing more.'

I helped raise her head and re-adjusted the pillows, noticing how thin her arms had become and the tremble in her hands. I felt an unusual urge to hold her as tightly as I could.

'Mother are you all right?'

'Yes dear,' she said faintly.

Her eyes opened wider as she slowly came to her senses.

'Why are you here, Annie?'

'To visit you Mother. And I would have brought some of your favourite geraniums but the flower seller was not in the town market today and I'm afraid Mrs Byrne had pruned the last of the garden blooms a few weeks ago.'

I held a glass of water to her lips. 'Do you feel unwell?'

She blinked. 'I am not in terrible pain.'

'Good,' I replied, noting the slur in her elocution.

'You are a good daughter to me, Pixie. Annie! Oh dear, I meant Annie. Good heavens, why did I say Pixie?'

I froze, my heart thudding in my chest.

'I am your daughter Annie. Look at me.' I tilted her chin upwards to face me. Her pupils dilated as she tried to focus on my features, the drugs probably making it difficult for her to do so.

'Yes of course you are, Annie, that's right. Who is Pixie then?'

'Pixie is your daughter too, but she is gone now Mother, she died many years ago.'

She stared at me blankly.

'And has your father gone too?'

I touched her hand. 'Yes. I'm very sorry.'

Her face crumpled and she emitted a loud sob.

'Oh Annie, do you forgive me now my dear?'

I shook my head in confusion. 'What must I forgive you for mother? For his death? We know that Father died of natural causes, it was not your fault or mine.'

'No, no...' she said shaking her head, 'not your Father, not him.'

'Well whatever do you mean?'

'For Pixie,' she wailed, grabbing the bed covering and throwing it aside as she attempted to rise.

'Mother, what are you doing? You cannot get up you are in recovery. The physician is on his way. I will have to call Bessie.'

'God no, I beg you. Don't summon that hag of a woman again. Please Annie, she poisons all my meals.'

I almost let out a laugh at her foolishness despite the real terror I felt at her shocking delirium.

'Mother where do you think you are going?'

She stood before me in a stupor, her shoulders sagging beneath the long thin white gown. I pitied her immensely.

'I did not mean it, I did not mean to do it, Annie.'

I took hold of her trembling hands.

At that moment Bessie walked in with bottles of tonics. She stood still in her tracks, shocked at the sight of Mother standing in my grasp.

'What did you do, Mother?' I persisted.

Her lips trembled as she tried to speak, slumping down on the bed.

'I did not mean it Annie, please believe me.'

Bessie stepped forward and placed the items on the table and took a syringe from her apron pocket.

'Hold her still Annie we don't want her blood pressure rising again.'

She lifted Mother's gown and slipped the needle into her arm.

Mother did not flinch.

'Annie... please... forgive me, you must... you...'

'Shush be calm,' I said, stroking her arm. Her chest rose and fell until she became limp and her eyes fluttered to a close.

'The physician is on his way,' Bessie said. 'Don't leave her yet Annie.'

'I will not leave her alone.' I reassured Bessie, even though fear travelled in sharp bolts through my body.

When the doctor's footsteps approached I hurriedly wiped the tears from my eyes, adopting a newly composed expression just as he stepped in to the room.

Twenty-Four

Leah

'Why did they refuse you?'

I cowered but it was too late. Elsie's hand struck my cheek sharply, the sting filling my eyes with tears.

'I did my best, honestly. The employer said that my skills were insufficient. I could do nothing more.'

I cried out as she slapped me again, glowering angrily before sitting back in her chair.

'I can't say I don't believe him. Coming from that orphanage where I've heard you spent your days skipping about in the grass. What sort of skill would you call that then? Ain't no use to anybody is it? Well don't keep expecting free accommodation here young missy, but you ain't getting off that lightly. You had better get back out there tomorrow and return with some work.'

'But I have enquired everywhere for the last fortnight.'

She raised her hand once more and I cowered beneath my shawl.

'Don't gimme any more of your lip you little brat. You'll go back out tomorrow and try harder. Feed 'em some lies if you have to but you'll come back here telling me you've found employment and I'll be in charge of your earnings when you do.'

I moved away from her filled with resentment. I had traipsed the length and breadth of town to secure work, but none was to be found. Elsie thought I could just snap my fingers and obtain any kind of position on a whim.

I would have escaped back to the orphanage there and then only I was certain Mrs Featherstone would sympathise momentarily, then make me return here again. I wish she could somehow see how mean and hateful Elsie was, and Father seemed far too afraid of his mistress to make a fuss.

Since my arrival I had scrubbed clothes, fed her children and performed every laborious task she or her eldest children had no desire to do. My hands were blistered and raw and many tears spilled on to them as a grudge silently grew within me.

Each night I curled up to face the wall and thought of Pixie, for I missed her dearly. I could only pray that she was not too badly affected by my absence.

That evening as I lay on the floor in the darkness I had great difficulty settling myself to sleep. The wind rattled the bits of torn paper which barely concealed the cracks in the window. A cold breeze came through it and chilled my bones.

I could hear Father's snores behind the thin layer of curtain that separated us and the occasional snuffle of the children as they lay piled together in the cot.

Sleep did not come easily though I must have drifted off because I was awoken by a loud knock on the door which I thought was still the wretched wind. Elsie stirred and cursed loudly.

'Who is calling at this hour? You'll wake up the bairns!' she complained loudly.

I glanced up and saw from the clock that it was nearly seven. Then the bed gave a creak and Elsie's feet could be heard padding to the door where a male voice spoke to her. He spoke so faintly I could not catch his words. She re-appeared to shake Father awake from his deep slumber and I felt my heart begin to race. What trouble could I have caused now? I slid deeper beneath the covers and tried to block new troubling thoughts from arising.

Father rose, and together he and Elsie spoke in hushed voices in the hallway as I lay in fear of what was to come. I hoped dearly that it was not some terrible news about Pixie or some unfortunate occurrence at the orphanage.

A few moments later Elsie came towards me with the large curlers in her hair bobbing wildly about, her face set into a tight grimace.

'Get up and pack your belongings,' she ordered.

'Why, where am I going?' I asked in bewilderment.

'Back to that bleedin' orphanage again. That's exactly where you're going.'

A stream of confusing thoughts struck me as the carriage made its way across the bumpy road and to the life I had been yearning to return to. Mr Hopkins had looked at me regretfully, remaining stubborn on the matter of passing any information when I had asked him why he had been sent for me. He only revealed that Mrs Featherstone had sent him with a message for my father, and he was to have me in his company when he returned.

How Elsie and my father had let me return so easily I could not comprehend. When I recall how adamant they had been that I leave in the first instance it seemed very strange that I was now making my way back.

But I cared not for Elsie and her brood, nor did I wish to ponder the circumstances too deeply for my only desire was to see Pixie again. I hoped somehow that Miss Jeannie was looking out for her, though I knew that she did not feel the same degree of affection towards her as I did.

The tall building came into view and seemed strikingly more handsome than the first time I had viewed it. More-so when we drove past the sun rising over an expanse of rich green hilltops and dew-covered fields. My first visit had been filled with fear. Perhaps I had not truly looked at the concrete structure before with such an appreciative eye. I was glad to see it now, believing just a few hours ago that I would never return.

Mrs Featherstone greeted me at the entrance. I longed to take the stairs hurriedly in order to see Pixie, but I dared not offend Mrs Featherstone who called me back to her office and told me to seat myself.

She looked kindly upon me as I settled into the familiar hard chair.

'We are happy to see you here again Leah, are you well? I hope your experience did not prove too distressing.'

I smiled in an attempt to hide the heavy pain in my heart as well as the blisters that had formed on my hands as I tucked them beneath my shawl.

'Father is much changed now,' I informed her. 'It seems that he does everything that Miss Elsie desires and shows no real affection towards me.'

She lowered her eyes. 'I am truly sorry. And all the more reason why we must pray for him. But I also expect that you are wondering why you have returned?'

My eyes opened wide. 'Oh yes, I did not expect this at all. I am so thankful and content to be here again Mrs Featherstone, why did you send for me, may I ask?'

'You are a very fortunate girl Miss Cunningham. A certain gentleman has acquired your services here.'

I stared at her with incomprehension. 'A gentleman? My services? But whom and why?'

'I also have some unfortunate news so please do not become too distressed.'

'It's Pixie isn't it?' I said, my heart lurching. 'Oh please tell me that she is not too badly affected.'

'Well I am afraid that she reacted to your departure negatively. She refused to eat and bit Sister Ernestine more than once. It was quite a task to control her and we were unsure how to proceed. She was certainly no longer the contented young infant that we witnessed in your care.'

I knew well how she could switch from being comfortable to distinctively defensive amongst those she did not trust. I had witnessed it myself the first day I saw her.

'I contacted Pixie's Father, whom you know has been here to visit his daughter before.'

'Yes, but I have no idea why,' I said. 'I thought it was not the customary practice.'

'It isn't,' she replied, shaking her head. 'But he somehow feels responsible for her welfare, that is all I can say. But even he was alarmed to see how quickly his daughter had declined once you left. We informed him that normally we would have to send such difficult children to a facility where proper treatment is warranted. He was saddened that you were gone and did not want this decision for his daughter.'

I sat quietly taking in the news, shocked by the fact that Pixie's father *did* seem to care about the welfare of his daughter, but it also seemed her mother did not.

'So how is it that I am here. Is that why you have brought me back? Why did Elsie let me go?'

'We discussed the matter and Mr Reinhart decided to acquire your services so that you could return to Pixie.'

'How?' I asked again, 'Elsie and my father were not willing to let me leave.'

I was no closer to understanding this strange arrangement.

'Mr Reinhart has offered a decent sum to your Father, Miss Leah. He will supply it in order for you to continue caring for Pixie. It is without a doubt quite an unusual arrangement. But I could see no reason to object. After all, you seemed happier here, as did Pixie. It would have been foolish for your father to decline such an offer.'

I nodded, thinking that it would have been Elsie who came to that decision, no doubt. She would be pleased to pocket the money each week directly and not have to keep me clothed or fed. A perfect arrangement.

'How could I ever thank him?' I asked.

Mrs Featherstone smiled. 'That isn't necessary. In fact I should not have told you, however I felt you had some right in knowing the truth. But do not become complacent. Things could always change in the future.'

'Yes, I understand,' I said. 'I am truly indebted to Mr Reinhart, but how is Pixie, please tell me that, I wish to know.'

'She is not in good form Miss Leah, I am warning you now. We feared this could happen. We all hope that you can bring her back to good health again.'

I felt utter dread at what I might find when I saw her. I was pleased that they appreciated my usefulness and could see how much the orphan had improved with my attention. I would have more expected to be cut off from her completely, or reprimanded for allowing a relationship to develop between us. But I was very glad to see that they acted favourably. It seemed to me that Mr Reinhart had intervened and Mrs Featherstone, being a kindly soul, relented.

'May I see her now?'

'You may do, Sister Ernestine has been informed of your arrival. Please resume your usual duties as from tomorrow Miss Leah, and I hope there is some improvement with Pixie in a few days.'

I was so anxious to see her that I absent-mindedly left my case behind in the carriage and went back to retrieve it, taking it to my quarters where I found some of Miss Jeannie's clothes lying on the bed in an untidy pile.

She was still here.

I disturbed my own neatly made bed by placing my case on it and removing my coat and hat. I then walked through the familiar corridors towards Pixie's room, exhaling deeply in the hope that I might calm some of the nerves that had been steadily building the entire morning. I fretted about how I would ever explain my absence to her? Would she even accept my affection?

The door was left slightly ajar and for a moment I thought Sister was inside, but peering in I saw that the room was empty and Pixie was lying on her bed. I entered cautiously. She faced the wall and I gently placed a hand on her arm hoping not to frighten her.

'Pixie? It's me, Leah. I am back' I said in a whisper. At first there was no response, then slowly she turned her head and gazed at me in confusion. Above her left eye was a purple bruise and her skin was sallow. She also looked much thinner than before. No wonder her father had wished for my return. I looked at her and wept.

'I am so sorry, I told her' leaning forward to take her in my arms.

Her body tensed immediately and she threw back her head and screamed. A deafening pitch, even louder than the wail she emitted the very first time I had touched her. I jumped back and placed my hands over my ears.

Sister Ernestine appeared at the doorway, she glared at me angrily.

'I see you're back. Why have you disturbed her sleep?'

'I merely came to check upon her,' I said feebly.

She frowned. 'I had warned you Miss Cunningham. I told you what would happen if you became too close to the girl. Now you can see that I was right. Just look at her!'

She pointed angrily at Pixie as if I couldn't see how frail and weak she appeared with her body facing the wall.

'But I had no choice in leaving,' I exclaimed, feeling tears prick at my eyes. 'It's not as though I wanted to leave her.'

'Oh I know that much, but had you not been wasting your hours on her every day, taking her on leisurely walks and making her depend on your presence alone, well, she mightn't have been so affected by your absence.'

'But Mrs Featherst...'

'Don't use her as an excuse,' she cut in sharply. 'I did not approve of this charade from the start. Mrs Featherstone is too lenient on the matter in my opinion. If I were running this orphanage you would not be standing in this room right now young lady.'

I gasped at her cruel words which struck me with force. I fled the room and stumbled into the hallway where I fell to my knees. There I would have stayed if I had not made every effort to compose myself and head back to my own room where I shut the door and fell into a heap on my bed. I sobbed for a long length of time. I could not understand what I had done that was so abominable. I had been brought back to the orphanage by Mrs Featherstone to renew my care of the girl and it seemed that Sister only wished to oppose it even more. I felt anger at being used, pulled this way and that, without my consent on any matter.

For how long I lay on my bed I did not know. I stared through the window at the streaks of grey clouds forming over the hills. It appeared that a storm was brewing and I had no knowledge of time passing at all until I heard the door creak open. Jeannie's face peered in through a gap.

'What has happened to you?' she asked.

I could not look her in the eye.

'Nothing,' I told her emphatically, wishing at that moment that I could disappear.

'Leah. You must tell me. I was informed you were returning and I am so glad you are back, but what has happened?'

She approached the bed and handed me a clean handkerchief where I sniffled and sobbed, embarrassed by my own foolishness.

'I do not know why I was made to return, for Sister is now very angry that I am here. Mrs Featherstone informed me that Pixie's father had arranged for my return. Did he come back to see his daughter?'

I looked at her in earnest, hoping for an answer, but her face looked downcast.

'I saw the man myself. He appeared somewhat distraught. I do think it is only the second time he has visited. And there were words spoken about you... about Pixie's decline and about the...'

She turned her head away so that I could not see her face for she must have felt guilty for eavesdropping again outside Mrs Featherstone's office.

'About what? Please! Tell me everything,' I begged.

'About the asylum. There was talk that she ought to be placed there where they are better equipped to control her unruliness. But I did not hear the entire conversation. At some point you were mentioned and then it seemed as if bringing you back here was the only alternative solution.'

I sniffed loudly. 'Well I *am* back, but she fares no better does she?'

'Why do you say that? Will please you tell me why you are so distressed?'

'I have just visited her room and she became hysterical. Sister witnessed it and had cross words with me. I am quite sure she is angry because I have returned.'

'Oh,' she said waving her hand. 'Sister is all bark and no bite. But I do agree that you are placing too much of your time and energy on Pixie, but it seems Mrs Featherstone allows it.'

'And what is wrong with that?' I spat vehemently. 'Why can I not make a small difference to just one unfortunate child, if I cannot make a difference to all of them?'

I began to sob again and she sat close to me.

'You can only make so much of a difference in this world Leah before it all starts to go black.'

'Black? What do you mean?'

'Yes, *black*. I mean the world, and everything in it. It is black isn't it? Our lives, everything around us. Our struggle to live day by day. Yet we are always searching for this light of God of which they talk about. The light that might lead us to an everlasting glory. But that is only in death, for in life there is nothing but darkness. Can't you see? I should know. I was planning a life with Jack and our baby and it was snatched away from me. The darkness always gets us in the end Miss Leah.'

She took hold of my arm and I pulled away, finding her bleak words to be hardly a comfort.

'I am sorry,' she said quietly. ' I have come through a difficult experience too.'

'Yes, I know that you have.'

'Will you forgive me?'

'For what must you be forgiven?'

'My thoughts on the matter. I know they aren't cheerful, but all right then... what if you accompany me to the village hall tomorrow? I would appreciate some company and we can forget all about our troubles. I think it would do you some good, you are now fifteen years of age and yet you act as if you are ancient!'

I frowned. Perhaps I *was* ancient. I certainly felt it, but the last thing I wanted was to abandon Pixie again, but then, perhaps I should exercise caution upon my arrival, especially under Sister's watchful eye. And maybe Miss Jeannie is right, I am far too involved in her emotionally which was also affecting my own health.

'She is bruised, she hurts herself, she must be so very unhappy,' I spoke the thoughts aloud.

Jeannie sighed. 'Bruises will go away soon enough, she will come round to you again, just give her time,' she said, standing to her feet. 'Look, you cannot take on all the ills of the world Miss Leah. Let us enjoy just one evening as normal young ladies.'

The words 'normal young ladies' sounded strange to my ears for I only knew of the life I had led and would never know if that could be considered normal, or otherwise.

She left the room leaving me to my thoughts. Rain tapped at the window and I heard the clattering sound of children's feet dashing to and fro in the rooms below, orphans rushing to don their nightclothes, say their nightly prayers, and retire to their dormitories.

Perhaps Jeannie and Sister were right, Mrs Featherstone was too lenient with me and I was too involved emotionally with Pixie. Perhaps I should learn to toughen my spirit and spend less time with her even though the very idea of it divided my heart in two.

Twenty-Five

Annie

Her smile was warm and welcoming, her cheeks rosy. A tall chiffon hat covered her jet black hair. I would judge her to be in her late thirties, certainly not much more. She sat in a corner of the modern café holding the newly fashionable slim cigarette between white-gloved fingertips. A large teacup was placed before her.

There was a sparkle in her eye. I noticed how she clothed herself like a lady who was always readily prepared to be introduced to someone important. The type of person who somehow always happened to look perfect *effortlessly* as though it were a natural part of her existence.

She caught my eye as I approached.

'I apologise. I arrived early,' she said, her voice a little deep and musky. 'Oh, no need to apologise,' I replied, seating myself opposite her. 'I have to thank you for agreeing to meet me at such short notice Miss Staves.'

Her peach coloured lips parted in a smile. 'Ah, well as soon as you mentioned the orphanage I admit I became somewhat curious. I mean the lady you mentioned was someone who meant a great deal to my father, so I can imagine that she must mean a great deal to you too.'

'She does, strangely enough' I said, willing my eyes not to mist up. 'It seems she was close to my sister, closer than I had been. She took my place in her life. It was all quite out of my hands at such a young age.'

I settled into the seat as comfortably as I could but my nerves felt raw. I was still reeling from the terrible quarrel with Matthew. He had not contacted me since his spontaneous departure. I presumed that he might be on the train returning to Cornwall, or perhaps still sulking in a rented room somewhere in the city. I tried to pinpoint the moment where it had all fallen apart between us, but I could not. Our perfect weekend just somehow seemed to avalanche slowly into a disappointing affair.

'It's important to you, isn't it? Whatever happened to your sister in there,' she cut in, interrupting my thoughts.

I cleared my throat and ordered an indian tea from an approaching waiter. 'Yes. We are twins. We will always be connected, no matter that she is now…'

'Gone? But she will never be gone, will she?' She stirred her cup slowly with a teaspoon.

'No,' I agreed. 'She won't.'

I liked her immediately. She had that way about her of understanding a person without the necessity of too many words. She could easily finish a sentence that you started. Some people were simply gifted in that way. I clearly realised that Matthew wasn't as tuned in to my deeper thoughts as I would have liked. There was always some kind of misunderstanding between us, or was it that we somehow struggled to be completely understood by each other. Perhaps our wants and needs had changed, or were just moving in different directions.

I felt the strain of it tug at my heart, and as I looked at this calm woman with a steady hand and composed features sitting before me I willed myself to put Matthew to the back of my mind.

At least for now.

I picked up a tiny cinnamon cake and nibbled delicately as I told her as much as I knew thus far regarding Pixie and the orphanage. She listened with genuine interest, stopping me only once or twice to remark on something.

When it was her turn to speak she lifted her case and drew out another slim cigarette, lit it, then leaned back in her seat. The café grew quieter and the atmosphere became less frantic as diners began to leave one by one. I let my shoulders relax, eagerly anticipating what Miss Staves had to share on the matter.

'My father was a military man Miss Reinhart. One of those focused and disciplined men who was set in his ways, stubborn and always brimming with stories of his experiences, always too happy and obliged to tell. But he was a difficult man to live with, for many years of my life were spent opposing everything that he asked of me. My mother was always just a touch afraid of him. She would back up his word even when she knew he was being unfair or overly strict.

'It wasn't until he was struck down with an illness that we actually began… what one might consider to be described as… an adult father and daughter relationship. But by that point I was married, had borne two children of my own and so

I was unable to travel too frequently to spend the time with him that I would have liked. '

I nodded, understanding all too well the complexities and struggles inherent within the family structure.

'In ways that I could not describe, this young girl from the orphanage, Leah Cunningham, somehow changed my father. It seemed impossible to me, but yet she did. It was as if she softened the *edges* of him. Mellowed him down. I think she was the reason that our relationship actually improved in those last years of his life. For the first time ever, he actually listened to me.

'When I visited the residential home he dropped his hard manner and paid attention to my words. He became more accepting, more open to my ideas, more understanding if you will. I think that the fact that Leah was not his daughter and he could not dominate her or expect her to follow his orders granted him the blessing of *humility*.'

'How long did Leah care for him?' I asked.

She took another long drag of her cigarette leaving a ring of pink at the tip and smiled. 'Four years, two months, and thirteen days, exactly. And then my father died. I know as I have the paperwork detailing her employment and subsequent dismissal.'

I gasped. 'So do you know what happened afterwards? To Leah I mean?'

She looked down at her jewelled hands. 'I'm sorry I do not. I heard she ventured north to seek other work, it is a trail that will cost you a lot of time and effort to pursue. But I do have something however.'

She reached for her handbag, unclasped it and brought out a package wrapped in plain brown paper, setting it on the table between us like some treasure that she had just unearthed from a cave.

'This is something I feel you should have. Leah gave it to him. I do not know why. She must have trusted him deeply. I kept it in a box with some of his belongings. But I think it should be passed on to you, Annie.'

I stared at the package wondering what on earth it could be, worrying that the entire room could hear the loud beating inside my chest.

'May I open it?' I asked.

'I would not object but it is very special. Perhaps you should take it with you instead and peruse it when you are alone.'

She glanced at her wrist watch.

'And I am also afraid that time has caught up with me. I must depart to complete some errands, but meeting you has been a great addition to my routine. I must thank you for contacting me. It feels almost coincidental. For this...' she touched the package gently... 'this could not have been given to a more deserving person. It was meant for you and I sincerely wish you and your fiancee all the best.'

I could only smile at her, as I felt too overwhelmed with happiness to speak.

'We must meet again for tea. Perhaps when I return from my brother's home in Exeter. I am taking a short trip to visit him and his wife and my newly born nephew.

'Wonderful,' I smiled. 'I am sure you will have a lovely time, and I cannot thank you enough. I feel as though I have been spoiled today. It almost feels as if destiny has played some part of this.'

She smiled. 'I have always believed we create fifty percent of our lives and the hand of God decides the rest.'

She stood and called the waiter over to settle our bill. As we walked to the door I noticed that it had begun to rain, when it had shown such promising sunshine. I did not remember to bring my parasol. I would have to dash back home as quickly as I could in the drizzle.

I slipped the package tightly inside my coat to protect it. I already knew it held something precious even though I had not yet laid my eyes on its contents.

'Do contact me in a few weeks and let me know how things have developed won't you?' she said as we shook hands at the door.

'I most certainly shall,' I said.

And there I let her go, filled with information about my own life and its purpose. I knew she admired me by the way she seemed so engaged, and she had made no hurry to leave for the past hour and thirty minutes.

When I arrived at my door Bertie looked at me reproachfully, mewing loudly; a complaint about being left locked outside in the rain. I opened the door and he circled my legs before dashing inside.

I could not delay myself to do a single thing as I threw my purse and coat onto the couch and carried the package to my desk. Outside the wind howled through the roof above me.

The paper was discarded hurriedly and inside a leather cover woven with intricate designs, though a little faded, stole my attention. I ran my fingertips over it. It looked like a diary. Worn a little at the edges, but not terribly worse off than it ought to be. My hands trembled a little as I lifted the cover and saw the handwriting on the first page.

This is the property of Leah Cunningham.

Dated this day the 10th February 1881 where I am fourteen years of age.

I turned the page and read the first entry.

Miss Pixie (or Primrose)

Pixie is five years of age, her eyes are a soft blue and I think she is very fair of face. Today she took a great degree of interest in an unremarkable stone which she held in her hand then passed back to me. I hope that she learns a lot more in the future and if she is slow to learn, I will be more than content to teach her.

I inhaled a sharp breath.

Some words were lighter in print than others, and the ends and beginnings of some sentences were smudged in ink as though Leah had set her pen down and moved on to another task before coming back to the page, or simply hesitated before continuing.

The words were fluid, practised, coherent. This was a *learned* girl, one who had obtained a little schooling and obviously written before or been shown the art of writing at some point in her childhood.

I closed my eyes and lifted the book to my chest, disbelieving that I had it in my grasp, that I was in sole possession of the diary which belonged to Leah Cunningham herself and included passages about *my sister.* Finally I would gain an insight into their time together through Leah's own eyes.

I was sentimental, breathless, and brimming almost to bursting point with a desire to share this great and precious discovery with someone else, but when I looked up I saw only Bertie curled up in the chair opposite, watching lazily and with limited interest.

It took every effort not to flick through the diary of which there must have been at least fifty pages. I wished to savour every single word, re-live every experience that she had encountered. I listened to the wind howl as I stared at the diary. I became lost in a stupor, carried away in a dream, realising that all the while, as Leah wrote day by day, she never would have known that my eyes would one day in the future rest upon her words.

Twenty-Six

Leah

'It is fine, Leah. Please stop twitching.'

I wriggled uncomfortably as Jeannie tugged at the strings at my back. I felt a great pressure rise in my chest, a feeling that my ribs were being crushed into pieces. If this were the sort of pain that women endured in order to attract a person of the opposite sex, I fathomed in that particular moment that I would much rather choose the life of a sad and lonely spinster.

The shapeless and ungainly smocks we wore at the orphanage at least gave me the freedom of drawing a decent breath, though I kept my mouth closed and raised no complaint for I did not wish to sour the evening and spoil Jeannie's hopeful expectations. I had agreed to attend the village hall in an effort to cheer my self as well as build on my friendship with Miss Jeannie. She had chattered on about the event so much in the past twenty four hours that I could hardly disappoint her.

'The dress will give you a womanly figure because all women know that a dress becomes the description of a person. And not forgetting the simple fact that the opposite sex likes a lady to look charming, and a sense of good taste is to be applauded.'

I scowled though she did not catch sight of it from where she stood. I cared little for the practice of raising my very modestly-sized chest for the pure advantage of male attraction. If a man were to ever find me pleasing I had always hoped it would be based on my desire to be loving and dutiful towards him.

'Oh you are a fidget. Well now, that is the best I can do. Turn to face the mirror and look at how vast an improvement I have made. I shall paint a dash of colour on your lips and then we are ready to leave.'

She swung me around like a ragged doll and dabbed at my lips with a pink velvety stick. I stared at myself in the mirror and admittedly felt something completely different to anything I had experienced before. There was a young girl staring back at me with pretty eyes, but with the soft frame of my mother, a much younger version of her. A lump formed in my throat as I came to realise in that moment how much I missed her, and this... the act of dressing for an occasion was something new and unfamiliar. I had the formation of a womanly bust where two small mounds of white flesh protruded beneath my chin and I suddenly felt alarmingly exposed.

'I cannot possibly venture outside like this,' I stated in a shaky voice.

'Why not Miss Leah? You are in the cusp of womanhood, what is it that you fear so much?'

I said nothing, for I knew that my words would not be understood, for she could not see the child that still resided deep within me, a child that clung to its fear of the future. Oh how much I dreaded the onset of adulthood. If I could remain a child forever I would gladly do so in order to save myself from the torments I had seen my own parents endure.

She stepped away from me and fussed with her own hair, attaching long clips behind her ears and raising it in a high mound only letting a few soft curls fall over her ears. She wore a similar dress, though the one she allowed me to borrow draped softly over my body in a bold purple, whilst her cotton dress was a mint green overlaid with a delicate flower design and finished with a small rose brooch her mother had once given to her. On her shoulders she had draped loosely a shawl in a contrasting grey.

'Where did you find these garments?' I asked, never having worn such a pretty dress before.

'I borrowed them from Louisa, she did not mind.'

'And who is Loui…'

'Shush now!' she said sharply. 'You ask too many questions. You must try to sit down in it for there are more layers to the skirt than you are used to.'

I began to pace the room in an effort to loosen the dress that clung to my chest as a second skin. I attempted to seat myself and found that my bottom would not reach the chair in the same manner that I was accustomed to and I promptly toppled on to the floor.

Miss Jeannie turned her head and let out a wild scream of laughter.

'Oh Miss Leah you will be the funniest thing this evening if you do not quickly learn how to conduct yourself.'

For my cheeks to blush any deeper seemed downright impossible. I frowned at her as she lifted me from the floor and handed me a small clutch bag to attach to my skirts. 'I will not be able to dance in this costume even if I wished to. Surely dancing itself is a very awkward thing and silly too.' I complained.

I felt foolish and inexperienced beyond words, wishing that I had refused this farce of a social evening.

'Have you never danced before in your life?' she raised her hands to her hips and stared at me directly.

'Not in any social aspect no, and I have never really conversed with a young man either, let alone danced with one.'

'Well do not fret so, there is a first time for everything. We will drink fresh lemonade and watch the adults on the stage. You will laugh so much at Mrs Murdoch's manner of dancing that you will forget about all your own nerves, but do at least attempt to walk genteelly if you can?'

I shrugged. 'I will try.'

We headed for the door.

'Oh, what time must we return?' I asked her.

'Mrs O'Flaherty says that we are to return before the stroke of ten or she will not allow us to attend ever again, but she will be fast asleep in her bed, you ought not to worry.'

'I just do not wish to wake up the entire orphanage.'

'If we arrive late we can always climb the fence to the ledge beside our room then steal inside the adjacent window, that is if you are worried about entering the main building and causing a racket.'

My mouth fell open in surprise. 'I see! So that is how you manage to escape and return at all hours of your choosing?'

She giggled. 'It does take a little practice, especially in such a dress as you are wearing.'

'Well, I would not dream of it Miss Jeannie,' I said, my face reddening.

She laughed and slid her arm inside mine. In that moment the age gap between us knitted itself closer together and Jeannie occupied a little place in my heart.

As we glided along the building in our fanciful costumes I dreamed that I was an ordinary girl living within an ordinary family. Miss Jeannie was my older sister and we were on our way to a pleasant social occasion. An unfamiliar stab of excitement and anticipation that I had not really felt before gripped me as we left the orphanage together.

The sun was low in the sky as we walked the half mile to the village, passing fields and ditches muddied with soil. At times I had to lift the hem of my dress in order not to soil it and the heels of my footwear were already becoming clod with mud and fallen leaves. Jeannie admonished me for not keeping to the middle of the lane, but she was much more accustomed to the route than I.

Thankfully the walk was fairly straightforward without many twists and turns. I judged that I would find my way back to the orphanage without difficulty.

After twenty solid minutes of walking I asked her if we could stop for a while but she pointed ahead to a bright light which shone from a square grey building tucked behind a tall row of trees.

'It's right there,' she pointed.

We approached to the distant sound of music and laughter, and entered the back door quietly. I immediately noticed how many of the men were dressed handsomely, and the women had adorned themselves with dresses of every species of flower including foxgloves, peony's and orchids. Some wore lace fringes to their dresses, others wore plain cotton, and the occasional silk scarf or shawl was carried elegantly in the crook of an arm. I admired their hats and the large feathers swaying in their hair.

A band of three elderly men sitting on a small stage played a slow pulsing melody.

'Oh I should have given this to you before,' Miss Jeannie said, thrusting a sheet of paper into my hand from a small pile on a table by the door. 'But do not worry about it now.'

I read the first few lines hurriedly.

REFUSING TO DANCE.

A lady cannot refuse the invitation of a gentleman to dance, unless she has already accepted that of another, for she would be guilty of an incivility which might occasion trouble; she would, moreover, seem to show contempt for him whom she refused...

GIVING A REASON FOR NOT DANCING.

When a young lady declines dancing with a gentleman, it is her duty to give him a reason why, although some thoughtless ones do not. No matter how frivolous it may be, it is simply an act of courtesy to offer him an excuse; while, on the other hand, no gentleman ought so far to compromise his self-respect as to take the slightest offence at seeing a lady by whom he has just been refused a dance immediately after with someone else.

I could not decipher the words well and blinked nervously, folding the leaflet away into my pocket. Before I could proffer any questions, a gaggle of females not much older than Miss Jeannie flocked around us, and one wearing a pink ribboned hat smiled at us with obvious scorn as she fanned her neck delicately.

She wore gold coloured earrings and layers of sparkling jewels above her chest. I felt completely out of place in her presence and I wondered if she was a girl with a peerage of some kind. I swallowed hard and shrank back a little. I had no idea that Miss Jeannie's family was acquainted with such well-to-do folk.

'Good evening Miss Jeannie, I am very sorry to hear of your recent misfortune, though I must say that I am surprised to see you here so soon.'

I gasped at that girl's boldness and instantly feared Jeannie's response but when I looked at her face she seemed placid and calm. The girl then cast her eyes over me where her expression showed one of pure distaste.

'And who might this person be?'

Jeannie slipped her arm inside mine protectively. 'This is Miss Leah Cunningham. She is my friend at the orphanage. We share a room together there.'

'Is that so,' said the girl, already having lost interest in us as she began to turn away.

The band switched to a more upbeat tune.

'Despicable girl,' whispered Miss Jeannie into my ear. 'That was Miss Jane Bates, her father is the master of Hereford Boarding School and her mother is... well, I will leave those details for another time.'

Holding my arm she led me on.

We shuffled past a group of people laughing loudly. There seemed to be a division between the noticeably better off circles of villagers along one side of the hall, and those who had done the best with what they could afford, seated on the other.

As if hearing my thoughts aloud Jeannie spoke up. 'Don't worry too much about the uppity village folk, they won't even talk to you. Stay close to me, it is a large building and there are activities and games in the upper quarters. All are welcome here if well-behaved, though I might warn you that not all of them are.'

She winked at me, as if she knew something I did not about the very subject of behaviour.

I looked around wondering if her 'Jack' was here or one of the other fellows whom she cavorted with that I only heard about in her wild stories.

A sudden pinch of anxiety gripped me as I feared being left alone. 'You won't go will you?' I pleaded with her as she dragged me to a table set with rows of tall quaint glasses and liquids of varying shades.

'Of course not.'

A lady handed a glass to me containing a yellow coloured fluid.

'Oh what is…'

'Drink it!' Jeannie laughed and swallowed two herself in quick succession. I swallowed the liquid and its bitter taste stung my throat making my eyes water.

'Your first taste of an adult beverage,' she laughed.

We walked through the crowd of laughing and chatting people to a corner, where two other young girls fully clothed in similarly fanciful dresses were seated.

They stared across the room with no particular enthusiasm.

Jeannie leaned into my ear. 'They are the Sorrell sisters, we call them the *sour* sisters. Always dreadfully hard to squeeze a smile out of either of them.'

I giggled.

The band began to pick up its tune and couples moved to the floor to dance. Men held the women delicately at their waists as their long thick skirts swirled about them. I particularly liked how some younger children clung to their mother's hem as they danced.

A young boy of no more than six years was standing behind his father and trying in vain to copy his footsteps. His little cheeks scowled as he tried to keep in time, then in frustration he threw off his hat and stamped it into the ground. His parents laughed at his behaviour.

It seemed as though everyone was filled with good cheer and lack of troubles of any sort. It was the kind of place you could forget your woes entirely, if you had any.

I began to relax into my chair despite the restriction at my chest, which at least held my shoulders back and left me poised with a feminine posture. Dare I say that I began to enjoy watching the crowd, pleasure of this nature being something I had only read and heard about in my mother's tales of her youth. I was beginning to enjoy the experience when suddenly from nowhere two young men appeared. They stood nervously before us, and for a moment I was gripped in a fear that they were about to request a dance.

I looked at Miss Jeannie but she wore a playful expression, one I had not seen before and I supposed must only be reserved for the opposite sex.

I thought for a moment that I should study the leaflet inside my pocket, barely remembering now what it said... *was I unable to refuse a dance or was there a certain method to the refusal?*

Filled with dread I found I could not utter a word and was glad no-one could hear my heart thump wildly above the music.

Jeannie promptly stood up and shuffled on to the dance floor with the red-headed boy leaving the taller, dark haired lankier figure standing awkwardly before me. He pointed to the chair beside mine. 'May I?' he asked without meeting my eyes.

'Yes,' I said meekly.

He sat beside me, cheeks flushed crimson and bearing a serious expression.

'I have never seen you here before. I would ask your name if you don't think it rude of me.'

I looked away shyly. 'My name is Leah,' I said, the words coming out of my mouth in an unrecognisable tone.

'A pleasure to meet you Miss Leah, would you care to dance with me?'

Before I could refuse a hand was held out for me to accept.

'Oh I would, but I have never danced before,' I said, fear gripping me. 'I mean, not like this.'

He gave a cheeky smile. 'I understand. But if you dance right now, you won't be able to say that sentence ever again will you?'

I stared at him. It was certainly an odd remark to make but I supposed he was correct in his way of thinking. But should I accept the offer and risk fooling myself in front of every person present?

Bravely I stood, surprising myself and the poor fellow beside me.

I placed my hand in his and he led me to the floor, his eyes looking away as he slid an arm to my waist, which gave me a strange and uplifting sensation that I had never experienced before.

He raised one hand and I copied the same pose which other ladies obtained and placed a hand lightly on his shoulder. We slowly moved around the room and I prayed that I would not foolishly step on his feet. After a few moments I fell into his rhythmic movements quite well and we comfortably danced around the floor together.

'You see,' he said eventually, 'you are a natural dancer Miss Leah.'

I smiled and for the first time noticed an attractive glint in his green eyes.

'I did not ask for your name, how rude of me.'

'Mark,' he replied. 'Is this your very first visit here?'

'Yes, I came accompanied by Miss Jeannie, she comes often I believe.'

'Well I hope she brings you back again,' he said, his eye catching mine. It was then I realised a feeling of mutual interest between us, a certain warmth. I became aware again of my protruding chest above the hemline of the dress. My cheeks flushed.

'Are you all right,' he said, noticing my sudden discomfort.

'I am, but I think I need some air.'

He led me outside where a few people sat looking up at the sky and the many stars which shone down that evening. He pointed to two empty chairs and we walked over to them.

'Mark,' I began to say sincerely… 'I doubt I will return here again. I am mostly here for the sake of appeasing Miss Jeannie. I am not much interested in social occasions.'

'Neither am I,' he replied, before I could continue.

'Oh?' I raised my eyebrows.

His expression was serious. 'My parents always want to bring me along. Why they do so I cannot fathom. I would much rather stay at home and read my books about science.'

'You can read too?' I said, and he eyed me strangely.

'Of course, why would I not?'

'Oh no reason really, it's just such a privilege isn't it? I am not a brilliant reader, but I do try. I was afforded some weeks of learning thanks to my aunt.'

'What do you like to read,' he asked with sincere interest.

I dipped my chin shyly. 'Well I have never owned more than one or two books and I rarely have time now. I believe my mother would be proud of me, I write frequently,' I said honestly.

'Would be?'

'She passed away nearly two years ago.'

'I'm very sorry to hear that, though I think you are right, she would be proud,' he said.

'Where do you live?'

'I am staying...'

At that moment Jeannie appeared with two girls and one other boy at her side. They looked to be about Jeannie's age, surely no more than seventeen. I shrank back in my seat.

'Will we continue our game this evening?' one of the girl's said to Mark. His face flushed as she threw me a contemptuous stare.

'I await an answer?' she added impatiently, hand placed on her hip like a mother admonishing her son. Slowly he rose from his seat and Miss Jeannie came forward with a glazed look upon her face. I hoped she hadn't consumed too much.

'Come with us,' she beckoned.

'Come where?'

'Ssh, you'll see, don't be afraid,' chuckled the freckle-faced girl enticing us to follow.

They took a route around the side of the building through a bramble weed path until we reached a fence only waist high. I trembled, for I knew that whatever 'game' the group were engaged in, it was very likely secretive and not permitted.

The two boys jumped over the wire fence first and then turned to help the others. I arrived last, and Mark waited a moment for me to compose myself. I gingerly lifted the hem of my skirts, flushing with embarrassment, and took his hand placing my foot on the lower part of the fence. I leapt over snagging the bottom of my dress on a nail and tearing it as I did so.

Jeannie looked back and rolled her eyes.

'You will have to darn that yourself when we return,' she said in annoyance, but instead of stopping or assisting me she continued on with the others. They ran ahead together, pushing low branches and leaves aside, continuing down a small hill which opened on to a lake.

'Let me assist you,' Mark said. 'It is dark.' He took hold of my arm.

'Why are we here?' I asked, but he simply shrugged. I nervously followed until finally they stopped beside a log and the three girls stood in a circle.

'Jeannie, you start off,' said the tallest of the girls, who wore a long patterned skirt and blouse. She looked very serious as she guided Jeannie to the centre of the ring. Mark quietly urged me to join them and I tried to stop my arms trembling at my side. I had no clue what sort of game this was so I could only pray that it wasn't anything dangerous or humiliating.

Everyone held hands and began to spin in a circle. I peeked through closed lids and saw Jeannie. She had her eyes closed and was spinning and chanting in the centre of the ring in the opposite direction to the rest of us.

"Turn, turn, turn around, we must all close our eyes...

Who will I surprise, who will I surprise..."

She then stepped forward and tapped the boy on his shoulder.

'Nooo, not me first again!' he laughed.

The girls giggled and sat on the tree log.

I held my breath to see what was to come next, and then he began to remove his clothing as the girls held each other and screamed with wild laughter.

The moon was large and bright. I was shocked to witness the boy standing there in his undergarments. One of the other girls also began to undress, removing her print dress and remained in her petticoat and bloomers.

'Plunge into the lake. Now!' Jeannie laughed.

I stepped backwards, horrified. This was a game of strip tease, and I had been fooled into participating.

I grabbed Jeannie's arm roughly.

'You do not think that I am going to remove my clothing here in the presence of males do you?'

She looked at me resentfully.

'There are no adults here to stop us. It's just a little amusing entertainment, why must you be such a spoilsport?'

I tightened my lips angrily. 'I shall find my own way back to the orphanage.'

She gripped my arm. 'Miss Leah you cannot go back alone or you could get lost. And if you return to the orphanage without me I shall be in trouble if Mrs O'Flaherty finds you alone.'

I stared at her with incomprehension. Shocked by her foolish desire to bring me along without my consent, and then only to indulge in a humiliating game… and with boys too! I looked past her shoulder to see that three of them were already in the lake, laughing and splashing under the moonlight.

'That is your choice Miss Jeannie, but I am leaving right now,' I said finally.

I turned to look at Mark. He was standing to one side with his head lowered. I could see he was most uncomfortable too, probably only urged on by his male companion. 'Would you kindly escort me back to the hall?' I asked him.

He opened his mouth to reply but Jeannie pushed him aside.

'He will not,' she said stubbornly. 'You can wait another twenty minutes and we will all return together. No-one will miss us, they are all too busy dancing the waltz by now.'

Angrily I brushed past them both and continued to walk in the direction we had come. I heard Jeannie calling after me but I refused to turn my head. There was no sign of anyone behind me so I focused on making my way through the narrow path that would take me back to the hall at least, from there I would be able to navigate my way back to the orphanage without too much trouble.

Thankfully I saw the light from a window peeking through the trees now and then, it guided me sufficiently, but instead of entering the building I re-traced my steps back to the orphanage.

Along the way I felt sadness and then anger at Miss Jeannie and the way she had used me just to attend the village hall in the first place.

I was merely a pawn in her hand, a puppet put to use as her companion. I had heard her complain many a time that Mrs Featherstone no longer wished her to leave the orphanage alone, especially late at night when she was accustomed to breaking and entering at whim. This being prior to her recent loss, which seemed not to have softened or mellowed her temperament at all. Miss Jeannie, it seemed, had sprung back to the wilful and stubborn girl she had always been.

I reached the orphanage and took the key from my pocket to turn the iron lock in the gate. I would have sprinted across the grounds had I not been restricted by the clothing I wore.

When I reached the side of the building I opened a door at the back entrance and quietly climbed the steps up to my room.

It was quiet, not much could be heard save for a breeze rattling the window or groans and creaks from old floorboards.

Tomorrow, I decided, I would begin the day by taking Pixie on another walk through the gardens. I would pour every effort I had into making her happier again in-between my other duties. I would do this for her father, and even for the remainder of her family, (if she indeed had any,) even though they would never witness my efforts or the result of my actions.

Once I reached my room I was too filled with nervous energy to sleep. I quietly lit a candle and decided to log my thoughts. The candle stub flickered in the dark as I wrote a few lines. I carefully snuffed it out at midnight and lay back with a thankful relief. It would soon be dawn. I then wondered if Miss Jeannie had removed all her garments too and jumped into the lake to cavort about foolishly.

I thought of Mark. He seemed to be an honourable fellow that had been taken along against his will.

You are old and boring Miss Leah, I imagined Jeannie's voice suddenly taunt in the darkness. I scowled, closed my eyes, and let sleep claim me.

I slept so soundly that night that I did not even hear Miss Jeannie climb through the unlocked window in the early hours of the morning.

Twenty-Seven

Annie

You love your daughter.

I saw it when I looked at your face.

It was the day I watched you walk out of her room.

In any case, Sir, I can only thank you within these pages, not in person, for I know you would never wish to talk to a girl as lowly and uneducated as I. I could ask you questions, for I have so many, but I know I would receive no appropriate answers and of course, how impertinent would it be to intrude on your private family matters?

I would surely be expelled from here and with good reason.

There has to be a reason why your wife does not

visit her daughter. I am sure there is a wife and a mother, maybe even a brother; or a sister perhaps?

Why did you abandon Pixie here, Mr Reinhart? She is very clever and she plays often with me. If you could see her softened gaze, and the way her eyes light up when I enter the room, you would see that she deserves more than what fate has afforded her. You would see the way she communicates earnestly with her eyes alone. She offers so much, compassionately, sensitively and with loyalty.

I turned the page.

It was an outline of a bird, childishly drawn. I smiled.

I could not stem my tears from flowing. The girl possessed no shortage of generosity, but to think that my own father had visited Pixie as a child without ever informing me at all seemed like such a treacherous decision. He could have taken me with him to the orphanage, and if that were against all possibility, he could, at the very least, have told me how she was faring there.

There must be a reason why your wife does not visit her daughter.

This sentence infuriated me. It tore at the same gaping hole in my heart. Even Miss Leah had been wondering the same things as I. After all these years I could not understand why my mother never wished to see Pixie again and I was so angered I decided I might ask her outright.

I could do it after her early dose of medication, when she would be less likely to become anxious. Though it would likely illicit a slurred and unreliable response plus her fragility would be tested with my cutting words. I would have to accept her reaction or guilt would rise within me.

I put the diary to one side and sought Mrs Byrne whom I found polishing the crockery in the kitchen.

Mrs Byrne had been in service to our family for many years, I fathomed that she must have committed many details to memory. I had never provoked her on any matter regarding Pixie before, for it was disrespectful to do so. Servants should never cross the line of duty by discussing their employers' affairs publicly, and more especially with employers themselves.

Her back was turned to me as she held a ceramic cup.

'Mrs Byrne, do you remember the day that Pixie left us?'

She froze, letting go of the cup. It fell and smashed to the ground.

'Oh my goodness,' she exclaimed shaking, and promptly knelt down to pick up the broken pieces, her eyes avoiding mine.

I walked towards her. ‘I am sorry, I did not mean to alarm you.’

‘No, no madam, it is quite all right.’

We knelt together on the floor and I took her hands in mine. I spoke deliberately and quietly.

‘I wish to know what happened that day Mrs Byrne. I have been kept in the dark long enough. You were there. I recall that you came rushing up the stairs to instruct Miss Tilda to lock the door and detain me inside my room. The commotion downstairs it was… well it was terrifying to hear. Doors banging, Mother wailing and screaming. Then after some time all went quiet and a carriage arrived to take Pixie away.’

There was a long silence between us then she gathered the broken pieces and finally stood to her feet. I waited, hoping she would provide a crumb of information, but she nervously began to sort through the pieces, wrapping them in some paper.

‘I can glue them all together if I take them home with me, Miss Annie.’

‘Please,’ I begged. ‘Tell me.’

She looked at me intently.

‘Yes I saw it Madam, but I cannot speak of it, for it would be a grave sin to betray the trust of my employer’s whom I have pledged my loyalty too for the past thirty years. Please don’t ask that of me.’

I let out a weary sigh. ‘Father is gone now. And Mother is…’

'No,' she cut in, her hands trembling as she wrapped the pieces as carefully as she could manage.

'Your Mother is still with us, Lord have pity on her, and it is her duty to tell you the course of events, not me Miss Annie. It would be a sin for me to go above her word.'

She wiped a tear from her eye.

'You may be excused now,' I told her gently and left the room.

There was little point in upsetting her further for she had made a decision from the outset to remain loyal and sincere to my parents even though her service to them had ended some years ago.

In the study, I relaxed into my chair and flicked ahead a few pages of the diary. A new chapter caught my eye.

I am not sure I trust her words any longer. She can so easily be led astray and the way she tries so hard to persuade me to do things I feel uncomfortable about, this causes me much anxiety.

I also fear that she is right and that I am as dull as she predicts. But we are so different Jeannie and I, yet in-between all those differences we seem to remain friends.

I closed the diary. I should not have skipped ahead. It felt dishonourable to rush through such a precious record of her life.

A shadow passed by the door and I looked up. Mrs Byrne stood in the doorway with reddened eyes. She held the broken cup in one hand.

'Your mother blames herself for Pixie's accident Miss Annie. She needs to confess something to you before she dies. It will help ease her troubled soul.'

With that she left and shut the front door quietly behind her.

Twenty-Eight

Leah

'Please come,' I called to Sister.

'She laid down a pile of sheets which she carried in her arms and followed me to Pixie's room.

After removing Pixie's clothes to wash her I discovered several marks on her body that I had not seen before. Mottled yellow and purple stains marked upon her skin.

'She's been throwing herself out of the cot bed,' Sister said, as she inspected her body.

The marks looked sore.

'Pixie, why have you done this?' I asked.

She ignored me and clutched her doll tighter to her chest. Ever since I had returned she had barely looked at me for more than a few seconds. My heart sank. How was I to ever regain her trust? Her body appeared weak and still she did not care to eat more than a few spoonfuls of broth a day. One would think she was a girl of just two years by the size and weight of her.

'I will take her outside for some air,' I told Sister, who scowled at me.

'Did you finish your tasks in the laundry room this morning?'

'Yes,' I said, knowing that she would find reasons to prevent me from leaving.

'And where did you find these books?' she asked

'In the basement, I have been reading them to her.'

She tutted. 'Wasting time again. You know she cannot appreciate the words.'

'Her favourite is, 'Little Lord Lucas Visits The Circus.'

She picked up the book and leafed through it. 'Filling her head with nonsense.'

She then dropped it onto the bed, raised a few more complaints then left the room.

I carefully finished dressing Pixie then strapped her into the chair, placing a warm blanket over her shoulders. The wheels squeaked as we went. They most likely needed replacing though I dared not kick up another fuss.

'Come, let us go and see the nesting mother blue finch, how she is faring, perhaps she has already laid her eggs.'

I positioned her in the corner of the garden near the stone seat that faced a hedge. Tucked within it the blue finch's nest poked out between a clump of brown autumn leaves.

This time I had brought my diary with me. I had come upon an idea the previous night which I thought might cheer her. I turned a page and roughly outlined the bird as well as I could manage. I held it up to her face though she barely glanced at it.

I leaned towards her, took her small hand in mine and balanced it on the paper.

'Look Pixie, you can write with me.' I told her.

'I am Pi...' we wrote together in a scrawl.

She snatched her hand away and pushed her thumb between her lips.

I sighed, closed the diary and slid off the bench to kneel before her.

'Pixie I did not mean to leave you. I shall never do it again. It was not my fault, so please believe that I am being truly honest with my words. It was my father you see, and his mistress, they came for me and insisted that I live with them. I was unable to stop him. But your fa...'

I stopped myself. What good would come of mentioning Mr Reinhart. He had not since returned to check on her welfare.

'Can you show me some sign that you understand me?'

She stared at the ground with disinterest.

'I shall take you back, it is time for your lunch then a nap. And I hope you do not bang your head on the cot bed again.'

I fed her a soft boiled egg with a small cup of milk and left her in her room to sleep.

On my way to attend to other duties I passed Jeannie in the lower hall. She was accompanied by several children, each carrying a wide basket filled with autumn fruits, their mouths and shirts stained a deep red.

Jeannie and I had not communicated with each other since the incident at the village hall. I saw how her face dropped when she saw me which caused a pang of grief in my heart, yet I tipped my chin upwards and proudly and walked on.

In the laundry rooms I assisted two elder carers in emptying buckets of water and re-filling them for washing purposes. I then made my way to assist with the orphans.

More than two hours had passed when I returned to Pixie's room and found her lying on her side still clutching the cloth doll. Her hand was balled into a tight fist with something inside it. When I opened her fingers gently I saw that it was a torn page from the reading book Sister had carelessly thrown on to the bed.

'Oh dear, have you been tearing up the pages in the book? Pixie that is not a respectful thing to do, books are precious things and very...' My words caught in my mouth as I unfolded the page and stared at it with horror.

She had torn out the page of an inked illustration of Little Lord Lucas kneeling beside his younger sister's grave. His head lay on his mother's knee as she sat before the tiny mound of earth, crying into her palms.

In the story itself, Lord Lucas's father had taken him on a trip to the circus to help him overcome his grief at the loss of his sibling.

I flicked through the book. Every other page remained in tact.

I stared at Pixie and could find no appropriate thing to say. I stared at Pixie and could find no appropriate thing to say. She could not speak and so I could not fully determine her thoughts. My instinct was only to reach out to her, and this time she did not stiffen her little body, though nor did she lean in to me affectionately as she once used to.

I was disturbed by her actions and thought perhaps I ought to inform Mrs Featherstone, but I hesitated. What if she found the act disturbing and called upon Pixie's father, and he then decided she was best placed in an asylum?

My head reeled with confusion and the despair it had now created clung to me for the rest of the day. I could not repair the page in the book so I took it to my room and stared at the image for the longest time in an attempt to make sense of the illustration, and what it was that had caused her to rip it away and hold it tightly inside her hand.

Later that evening as I was helping in the scullery, Miss Jeannie entered looking flustered. She stood beside me and I knew she wished to talk so I sat on a chair to face her.

'I know what I did was wrong, and you have every right to be upset with me. I clearly see my wrongdoing now. Will you forgive me?'

'I am still hurt. You know that it was deceitful trickery,' I told her.

She nodded. 'Yes. I am sorry. It's just that, well, Mark is very fond of you.'

'Fond of me, what do you mean?'

She drew in close and lowered her voice to a whisper even though we were alone.

'He hopes to see you again very soon.'

I studied her face. I had no way of knowing whether she was lying or whether her words were true.

Her eyes did not leave mine and I felt suddenly uneasy.

'Will you come back to the village hall? It will be much better. You cannot say it was all terrible Miss Leah. And I promise not to misbehave again,' she begged.

I scratched my head thoughtfully, for I had enjoyed some parts of the evening, but my trust in Miss Jeannie had been impaired. I was not quite ready or willing to repeat the same event.

'No Miss Jeannie, I do not wish to return. Maybe in the future I will. There were some pleasant moments throughout the evening I do admit, but Pixie is unwell and needs me now.'

There was a moment of silence where her cheeks gained colour, then she stood to her feet, placing her hands on her hips like an impetuous child of four.

'Just as I predicted, the dullest girl in the world is YOU Miss Leah Cunningham. Now who am I to attend the village hall with, for Mrs Featherstone will not let me out of this orphanage alone at night.'

I remained calm in light of her outburst.

'I think it better that we do not bring up the subject of the village hall, at least not for now. Especially if accompanying you there is all that my friendship is based upon.'

She gasped. 'How could you say that? I asked you along to cheer you. You know full well that statement is not true.'

'Do I Miss Jeannie?' I said.

She backed away a step.

‘I cannot believe you think that of me, Miss Leah. You have hurt me immeasurably with your words. I must go.’

She walked away and left me staring at the cloth in my hand. Somehow I felt no remorse over my words and seemed to have found a new strength within me. Was this what my mother once said was the beginning of adulthood? That you could bear terrible things which you could not do so as a mere child?

That night, before I slept, I took another glance at Little Lucas and his grieving mother, then folded the page twice and placed it inside the diary. Sister Ernestine and Mrs Featherstone had asked to speak to me the following morning. I dreaded the very worst for I had failed to help Pixie recover sufficiently.

I tossed in bed in the dark, dreaming once again of toothless beings and dark hooded entities chasing me. Even in my sleep I fretted at how I might prevent Pixie from being taken away to the asylum. I had made a promise to her, and I could not go back on it. I was hopelessly attached to her and yet, for all my attempts at pleasing her, none seemed to make a difference.

Twenty-Nine

Annie

'She's quite sharp of mind today,' Bessie announced as I entered the room. 'Ooh flowers. She will be pleased. I'll fetch a pretty vase.'

Mother was sitting by the window, something I had not seen her do for many weeks.

'Flowers for me Annie? How thoughtful of you.'

I placed the wrapped bouquet on the bedside table and sat opposite her. The curtains had been opened fully and the sun was tinted orange across the horizon. It shone onto her face accentuating her features, but not in a terribly flattering way as it only highlighted the lack of colour in her hair, the dark circles framing her eyes, and the bony structure of her frame.

But some new aura of energy surrounded her which I had not seen for a long time as she smiled at me. I tried to think of a reason why she felt that today was the day she wished to leave her bed and sit near the window, for she always complained that looking out at the world only reminded her of her own entrapment.

Had she recalled an anniversary of some kind?

Perhaps a birthday she remembered?

Had she dreamt of my father? Did he come to her and speak in that mellowed voice he reserved only for her? The one he adopted when her nerves were about to tip her over the edge.

'How is Matthew?' she asked. 'Wasn't he supposed to be with you?'

I swallowed hard. I had been avoiding the inevitable confrontation with Matthew. He had tried to call several times, and each time I found some excuse to delay him, setting up a hard wall around my feelings. It was something I realised that I had become proficient at.

'He is well Mother, but very busy these days. He regrets he is unable to visit. I shall pass on your regard.'

Bessie entered the room holding a diamond cut glass vase. 'This will look lovely,' she said placing it on the table. 'Now Mrs Reinhart, be careful you don't knock it over now won't you?'

Mother did not respond.

Bessie left and I began to unpack the daffodils and arrange them carefully.

Mother sighed loudly. 'And what of this engagement Annie? The big wedding plan. You do realise that you are now thirty five years of age, that really ought to concern you. If you do not marry soon, well I fear that you will never raise a child.'

'Twenty-nine, Mother, and there is no need to be concerned,' I cut in, already feeling an irrepressible desire to leave.

'Ah yes, of course. We are much used to this conversation Annie, I know. I never get anywhere on this matter do I? Poor Matthew whatever did he do to deserve this poor treatment.'

And what did Pixie do to deserve you? I thought.

'Well if we get nowhere there is no need to bring it up again, is there?' I said matter-of-factly, focusing my eyes on the flowers and carefully plucking away wilted leaves from the base of the stems.

The tension had been set and the few minutes of silence which followed were broken when a lady knocked lightly on the door. She opened it a fraction, parking a service trolley in the gap.

'Would you care for a cup of tea, Mrs Reinhart?'

'Not now,' said Mother, her eyes fixed ahead absently.

I walked across the room to a drawer and opened it to locate a pair of scissors to trim the stems. A bottle of blue pills lay there. I read the label without touching them, noting that she would have been given them just before I arrived... *making her calm enough to ask about Pixie...*

I turned around to face her. 'Mother...' I began.

She had picked up a book and was flicking through it to find the page she had last read.

'Yes dear?'

'I must ask you to be honest with me about Pixie. No matter how awful you think the answer is, I wish you to tell me.'

She did not flinch though I spotted a small tremor in her lip.

'You may ask,' she said. 'In fact, I think it is time that we had this conversation.'

I gasped. She was actually going to confess without my encouragement. Maybe she *knew* that she was dying... and that if her confession could not be given to me now, it might never be revealed at all.

'Please, sit with me and hand me that glass of water. We do not want to be disturbed.'

I did as she requested and settled on the edge of the bed. She held the glass in a fragile grip. I held her hand and she let out a long weary sigh.

'In all these years I have never forgiven myself Annie. You know my fear of heights. You know it well. And so you know that I was the wrong person to witness her trapped up there.'

'Trapped?' I said.

'Yes.'

'She was trapped. You had gone inside the house. I had been in the drawing room when I saw you pass the doorway and ascend the stairs alone. I wondered where Pixie was but I spent a further ten minutes working on the painting. You know, the one you so loved. I was creating a replica for Father Craig.'

'The painting called, The Governess?'

'Yes, that painting, it was a gift to him for all his service and kindness to us over the years.'

'You never painted again after that day,' I said, 'and you have never approved of my love for the art have you?'

'I could never finish the painting nor ever paint a single stroke of a brush again my dear,' she continued, 'not after what happened that dreadful day.'

Her chin wobbled as she spoke.

'I cannot bear to see that painting, Annie. Anyway, I had put my brush aside and thought to venture outside into the garden. It was then that I spotted Pixie behind the wall. She had climbed the huge tree we had forbidden you both to climb. I saw that she was very high up and there were few branches from which she could take hold.'

'Oh Mother!' I gasped.

She squeezed my hand.

'I knew that she would either have had to jump down from her position, or climb a little higher to gain hold of the large branch that stretched across to the wall. I was overwhelmed with fear and so I made a rash decision. I gathered that if she were able to climb to the wall, from there I could assist her down safely.'

I envisioned the tall elm tree behind the wall and could see why Mother had thought of this plan. It did seem to make a little sense though I feared what came next.

'Why did you not call Father to help her?' I said.

'Oh heavens, I have asked myself that many times, Annie. Now when I look back I think I should have done so. But I wanted to prove that I could manage alone, that I did not need to run to your father for help every time something occurred. In any case I was glued to the spot with fear and time was not on our side.'

She took a sip of her water.

'I can also tell you that I was angered that she had disobeyed me. I shouted to her and she looked back anxiously.'

"Mother I cannot come down, help me," she said.

'I tried hard not to lose control as I stepped forward.'

"Climb further up," I told her. *"Reach one arm to the branch and from there you can crawl along it to the wall. Do as I say."*

'I could see the fear in her eyes as she implored me to help her. At first she did not move. Then I urged her again until she began to climb even higher. She was so far from the ground now Annie, but she only needed to reach to her left and take hold of that sturdy branch. But instead of doing so she screamed even louder and I became angrier and terrified.

"Just lean to your left and take hold of the branch," I screamed back.

'Finally she did as I asked and that's when she lost her grip and came tumbling down.'

Mother let out an anguished cry and brought her hands to her face.

I could not utter a word.

When she spoke again her face was dark.

'I failed as a Mother. I am so sorry Annie. I could never look into her eyes again. If I did I could only see my own guilt reflected back at me.'

'What happened, after she fell?'

Tears spilled on to her hands.

'I believed that she was either unconscious or that I had killed her. I panicked and could not calm myself. I did not have the courage to approach. I truly feared that she was dead. I ran inside the house and instructed Mrs Byrne to keep you away, telling her that Pixie had fallen from a great height.

'I called your father and we accompanied her to the hospital where we were to learn later that she was permanently damaged, that she would never walk again. The knock had damaged some portion of her mind too, for when she awoke she seemed not to remember or recall a thing but would only scream hysterically, or stare blankly.

'She would not speak another word from that moment on, her terror and shock was profound. You have no idea how much guilt I have carried around with me since the accident. It cut me so deeply. Oh Annie…'

Her sobs engulfed her, though I knew this would release a great amount of pain from her heart.

'Mother, I thought that it was the wall she had tumbled from, we all thought it.'

'That is what I told you, for I could not possibly live with the torment of the whole world knowing that I, her own mother, had screamed at her to climb higher, only to fall.'

I could have said many things to my mother in that moment, but I did not. I had achieved my aim of extracting the truth and it was enough. She was right.

The guilt she had carried on her shoulders all these years was more than enough to bear. Now I fully knew why she had abandoned her daughter and why she could never visit her again, not even to look at her face one more time, for Pixie would always be a reminder of her weakness, her inefficiency to cope with life.

She likely thought it was acceptable to let one child go because she still had another, sitting upstairs in her bedroom. The remaining daughter who knew nothing of what had just occurred to her sister, but was still young enough to forget about her over time.

'Did Father know the whole truth?' I asked.

'Yes, yes he did and so did Mrs Byrne, for I confessed it to her and she swore not to betray my trust.'

I marvelled at my housekeeper's devotion. And also my father's tenacity. Had he adored his wife so much that he would protect her reputation over his daughter's future?

'The physician told us that her life was forever impaired, that she was better placed in a suitable care facility. It was not my decision alone. We also wanted the best future for you.'

A part of me wanted to scream at her, *'Pixie could still have had a future. Even if you could not care for her at home, you could have still been a part of her world and not cut her off from us completely.* ***She was my sister!'*** But I was silent. I had only been given the truth after a quarter of a century. Nothing I could say to her could amend or change the past. *The loss of Pixie was unfixable.*

I stole a glance outside. It had started to rain. Her book lay on the floor and her hands lay limply on her lap.

'I do love Pixie,' she said. 'Though I know you don't believe that, Annie.'

A hard knock came at the door and Bessie peered in to inform us that the visiting hour had ended. I stroked Mother's arm in a brief show of understanding then picked up my purse and left the room.

Thirty

Leah

'I wish that I could be imparting better news Leah. I honestly do, but a decision had to be made. We are all concerned, not just for Pixie's own good, but yours too.'

My heart hammered silently in my chest as Mrs Featherstone spoke the words I had long dreaded to hear.

Sister Ernestine stood at the back of the room with her arms crossed over her chest in a hostile manner. I sensed that this ultimate decision had been influenced by her alone, as my affection for the girl had always been met with damning disapproval from the woman. It would not surprise me if Sister had also blamed me for Pixie's decline in health; she might have even influenced Mr Reinhart to end my association with his daughter.

But little good it would do now to make a conjecture based on my grief and without good evidence, or even to beg a reversal of the decision, for Mrs Featherstone had already made enough efforts in the past on my behalf.

My eyes stung with tears and for once I did not try to hinder them, but rather covered my face with my hands and allowed myself to cry.

Mrs Featherstone placed a hand lightly on my shoulder. 'I am sorry for this outcome Leah, none of us wished for it. You will have three days more with Pixie before she leaves us. Please do your best to make them count. Find strength in your faith and believe me that it is for the best. We can no longer help Pixie here.'

'Does her father know, was it his decision?' I asked.

'He has been informed of it,' was all she said, reaching for the door handle and ushering me out of the room.

There was nowhere I could think of to go but to *her*.

To tell her that I was sorry, once again.

To tell her that she was a wonderfully special young child.

To let her go with these thoughts imprinted in her mind, and most importantly, to let her know that she is *loved*.

We were permitted to spend the afternoon together in the gardens. I pushed her chair slowly across the same path as if I could slow the passage of time itself, only occasionally stopping to collect fallen leaves and berries from the hedgerows. Mounds of them had been brushed into piles as I wheeled her past them, pointing out the newly laid chicks a mother finch hid inside her nest. Their tiny bald heads poked out on long necks as their beaks snapped and squealed hungrily for food.

Pixie's sad expression did not change.

Nothing, it seemed, interested her. Bruises marked many areas of her arms and legs where I presumed she had persisted in rocking against the cot bed. Her eyes were sunken and dark, yet she sat with indifference to it all. From my pocket I withdrew the missing page from the storybook. I unfolded it to reveal the same image of Lord Lucas leaning over his mother's knee as she wept over her baby daughter's grave.

I did not hand it to her but placed it on her lap. I wished to see what reaction she might show.

She did not look at first as she sucked at her thumb. I thought she would not react at all, but then a shadow cast itself across her features. Her eyes rested on the page though she did not appear distressed, then she lifted her hand and placed it on the mound of earth, upon the grave of the young child itself.

She bore such a terrible sadness in her eyes as her hand rested there. I tore the page away from her lap and instantly she began to cry. She reached her hand for it again and I realised that she was trying to convey a message to me.

I drew her into a tight embrace. 'No, no, don't think that Pixie. Don't ever think that,' I said as I wept into her hair.

I rocked her in my arms for some moments, willing her to trust in something greater than what we knew stood between us; the heavens and this earth. Even though our time together was coming to an end she would never truly leave me.

She did not push me away.

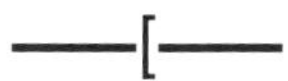

That same evening I lay in bed feeling hollow and emptied from all thoughts and feelings. I tried hard to cast aside the darker dreams which had haunted and chased me the past few nights. I did not want to think about the institution she was to be taken to and Mrs Featherstone did not confirm it outright to me.

But I knew.

Deep inside I knew.

At points I wondered if perhaps she truly would fare better there, although it was terribly hard to imagine so. She would surely continue to perish. She could not afford to lose any more flesh from beneath her skin and the healthy complexion she once possessed seemed a distant memory.

Late at night Jeannie entered the room. She shuffled about quietly laying her clothes out for pressing and tidying her bedside drawers. We were still not on speaking terms, but once she had finished her tasks I felt my bed springs creak as she sat beside me.

'Will we ever talk again?' she asked in a low whisper.

I had no will to respond.

I could not tell her that Pixie would soon be taken away. There was no need for her to know the reasons for my despair. She would find out soon enough from Sister.

'Sleep well Miss Leah,' she said and retired to her own bed.

I awoke the following morning drenched in a terrible sweat and when Sister arrived with clean sheets she snapped that I would face another illness if I did not compose myself.

'You aren't eating enough,' she told me emphatically at breakfast. 'Skin and bone you'll be soon Miss Leah if you don't eat right. What use will you be then? Start getting her out of your mind, there are other orphans here that need caring for.'

I made no reply to her callous comments as I sipped at my milk silently.

Jeannie then walked in to the kitchen and sat beside me on a little wooden stool. She tried to hold my gaze but I looked away.

'I know what is to happen,' she began, 'I wish I could help you. I wish you could see that some things happen for the best, even when we don't like them.'

I made no response and promptly left. I was trapped in a private anguish with feelings and fears that I could not express. The image of Pixie in better form, and when the possibility of happiness was within her reach, would not leave my mind. I had been so close to giving her that small measure of happiness that it crushed me to realise that I had failed.

It was not the end of Pixie and I, surely it could not be?

How could they all refuse to see that casting her out would mean the end of her?

Had she tried to tell me the little grave in the book was hers? And that maybe her own mother was the lady grieving beside it?

I stopped half way up the staircase as a new thought struck me with a forceful realisation.

Maybe she was telling me that she *wanted* to die.

Thirty-One

Annie

Bertie circled my feet, begging and crying for his meal but I could not tear my eyes away from the diary. I unveiled an illustration torn from a book tucked in-between two pages.

When I carefully unfolded it I saw that it was an inked drawing of a young boy wearing a small cap and sitting with his mother beside an infant's grave. It was particularly disturbing. The last few weeks of entries had shown a sad transition in Leah's thoughts. She seemed to have gone from utter devotion to feelings of despair and failure, starting from when she returned to the orphanage.

I was saddened by the passage where she wrote of Miss Jeannie's miscarriage and then the renewed promise of friendship that was almost rekindled later on, only to be hampered again by a quarrel at the lake. Many handkerchiefs became soaked with my tears throughout the course of the day as I took in her words of despair.

Even though I had read the last part of her diary many times, I could not help but return to one particular chapter. The words had now become engrained in my memory.

There was no longer anything recognisable within me. I had become an empty shell.

I carried a darkness so deep, so heavy and so grim, that it filled me with sadness. I could not even re-capture our joyous memories together or thoughts of a more positive nature, for my mind would only re-play the tragic news delivered to me over and over again.

Sister Ernestine, yes, I hasten to say this, but I would have quietly pointed an accusing finger at her. Perhaps the marks on Pixie's body were caused by her, but what good purpose would there be in asking? She would only deny any accusation against her.

And as for her death?

Well, the deed has been done.

Though I knew I had invited Sister's hostility since the day I arrived, she would likely have been the person to squeeze the precious life from my small angel, but no-one dare say it.

Not even I.

It would be like casting a stone without any evidence.

This sad morning when I was standing in Mrs Featherstone's office with several members of the orphanage staff, Sister cast her eyes at me as though I was the lowest born animal in a pen. If she had not instigated this dreadful tragedy herself, then it would not be surprising that she silently suspected me of doing such a dreadful thing. They all wished to know if I had entered Pixie's room the previous night and taken her life.

Mrs Featherstone appeared stunned. I was told to leave the orphanage. But I did not cry for I was very glad to go. There was nothing left for me here, not now that my dear Pixie had gone on to the Lord's arms.

The undertaker arrived shortly after nine.

He gathered her pitiful little body in a sheet, and with a sour expression he carried her away to the small graveyard behind the chapel. I hoped he would place her in a pleasant spot. The graveyard was a place I had always been too afraid to visit for there I presumed many orphan souls were laid to rest. I never wished to tempt death's desire to claim another tiny soul by taking Pixie there.

I was told to stay out of sight, preferably in my quarters, until further notice. Meals were brought to me and Mrs Featherstone added that she would summon me after a day or two.

Oh such a dreadful ache resides now within me. How will I survive it?

Dear Lord why did you take so innocent and fragile a human?

Jeannie consoled me today. I lay my head on her lap as she stroked my hair and I slept with the curtains drawn for many hours, or was it days? In a state of emptiness I lie here, praying fervently for her soul.

Downstairs the carriage awaits me. My belongings are packed and I am ready to leave. It was a comfort to me when Mrs Featherstone touched my shoulder gently.

My future is uncertain however, as this diary has witnessed my life with Pixie, so shall it end alongside her.

Leah Cunningham 17th October 1882.

These were her last words.

It seemed that after she had left the orphanage and began her position with Mr Staves, she decided that her life there had ended. All her words and thoughts from then on were likely either kept within her heart, or passed to the ear of Mr Staves himself. A man also deceased who would never be able to tell me how she fared in the aftermath.

Pixie had been discovered dead, having suffocated on some small item lodged in her throat. I was shocked by Leah's suspicion that it had been placed there.

Could Sister Ernestine have been so cruel as to end my sister's life that way? Was an orphanage carer really capable of such an atrocity? The act of murdering an innocent.

I could not possibly know. At worst, I pondered whether Leah herself was truly capable of something so final and harsh. Would she have done it to free my sister, to free her from the entrapment of a body that could not run, a mind that could not think?

My mind turned to the picture illustration.

A scene of death.

Leah suspected that this was what Pixie might have desired.

So could she have quietly killed Pixie reluctantly, lodging an item in her throat and leaving her there to perish? And that being the very reason she was sent away... to avoid a scandal... to hush any other suspecting individuals.

But many infants would have perished there frequently. Such things would not be questioned and the Lord simply took away the frail and the weak.

I tried to quell a sudden anger that Father did not inform me of her death. He would have been notified. I suddenly hated him for his desire to protect me by withholding the details all these years.

I closed my eyes tightly thinking back to my conversation with Miss Wakefield at Lowcroft Cottage. Then it returned to me.

'Alas, I do remember your sister with vagueness though I am afraid that I do not know what became of her. That is something I cannot

tell you as I had left the orphanage before she passed.'

Miss Wakefield was there! Was her own memory failing her?

Miss Jeannie Wakefield had lied.

My mind became burdened with troublesome thoughts. I set down the diary and decided to take a soak in the bath tub. My muscles ached from the reading posture I had adopted for most of that day. I had not managed either to finish the painting I wished to frame and place on the dining room wall.

It was the same one which Mother had been working on when she learned of Pixie's fall in the garden. The sun streaming in through tall windows as a Governess leaned back in a conservatory chair reading a book. I had chosen to replicate it, the luscious green grass surrounding the concrete white washed wall, the very one which I had grown up to believe Pixie had tumbled from.

But in my desire to change the original painting, I drew an outline of a young girl standing upon the wall wearing her favourite summer frock.

She stood poised gracefully with her arms above her shoulders, one foot *en pointe*, the other leg raised slightly behind her. The sun shone down on her shining curls which were wrapped loosely in silk ribbons.

In this portrait there was an expression of happiness upon her features.

There was no Pixie anxiously climbing a tree to reach higher, nor was she struggling to grasp hold of a branch before slipping to meet her sad fate. An act spurred on by her Mother to change the course of her destiny in moments.

It was just the darling sister that I remembered, captured forever in a scene of happiness and innocence above all else.

The telephone ring startled me as I was changing into a freshly laundered nightgown that smelled of lemons and spring scents, a fragrance Mrs Byrne had been adding to our night garments for many years.

I hurried to pick up the receiver and placed the speaking compartment to my lips.

I waited for the few crackles to disperse.

The operator passed a call through.

'Hello? Annie?'

It was Matthew.

'Hello dearest Matthew,' I said, feeling suddenly brighter hearing his familiar voice.

'Annie, look, I have had some time to think and...

My heart lurched at these words.

He was leaving me.

'Annie I want to move back to London, I think it would be best for us if I were closer. It's hard to make this work when we are so far apart, don't you think?'

I froze. The realisation struck me that I had been spending too much of my time chasing the past, one which should not be forgotten but perhaps laid to rest.

Dependable, patient and loyal Matthew had waited for me long enough.

'Yes Matthew. I miss you, and I want to start afresh.'

Strangely, I could feel his warm smile through the line.

The telephone crackled again.

'I will call again tomorrow, are you free?'

'Yes, I have one small errand to run tomorrow, then I will always be free,' I told him.

I remembered the first few weeks of communication between us. It was a little like this. A whirlwind of stolen moments sharing sweet words, quiet dates and unplanned chaotic and thrilling parties, sad partings and happy reunions. This had been our lives as we both tried to follow the plans we had laid for ourselves, yet, we also wanted to be together and achieve our potential to its fullest extent.

I replaced the receiver and made a mental note to place a call to Miss Wakefield after breakfast. After dimming the lamp I slipped into my bed clutching Miss Leah's diary in my hand.

'Thank you,' I whispered to her, hoping she was now in a good place, maybe with Pixie at her side.

That night I slipped easily into a restful slumber.

Thirty-Two

Annie

The tea Miss Wakefield poured into my teacup was of a weaker strain than the last. She had arranged three delicate coconut pastries on a side plate, but I informed her that my appetite had already been satisfied an hour ago.

I wished to come outright with my questions having made it clear that I would only stay for a short while, but I let her talk for some time of her own pleasantries and her actions in the women's suffragette movement, something she obviously strongly believed in. I noticed that her animation was lively, but on the subject of the orphanage her face would immediately take on a clouded view.

Gently I spread my fingers over the diary within my coat wondering what she would think when I confronted her with its contents. I finally found the opportune moment when she paused speaking to re-fill her tea cup, and changed the subject to ask me if I had returned to the orphanage in recent weeks.

'No, actually I have not,' I told her surreptitiously. 'I did however meet a person who formed some connection to the orphanage.'

She cocked her head to one side and raised an eyebrow. 'How interesting. Might I ask whom that is?'

I smiled. 'A lady called Miss Staves. It came to light that Miss Leah Cunningham assisted her father for some years until his death.'

She paused with her teacup raised to her lips. 'Well that is something I did not know. As I said I had already left the orphanage much earlier than she...'

'Please stop there Miss Wakefield,' I said firmly.

She seemed taken aback by my tone and I reached into my bag for the diary placing it on the table between us.

Her expression changed into one of shock.

'Do you recognise this?' I asked.

Her hand began to tremble and she put her cup down on the table spilling its contents on to the saucer.

'I do recognise the cover. It is Leah's diary.'

I nodded.

'Yes, it was placed in the care of the family Leah pledged her service to. Inside it Leah testified to your presence at the orphanage during the time of my sister's death. You even saw Leah to her carriage on the morning she departed. So could you please explain your deceit?'

She looked away.

'Why did you lie to me Miss Wakefield, for what possible reason would you feel the need to be dishonest?'

There was a few moments of silence where only the subtle ticking of the pendulum clock could be heard.

'Miss Wakefield,' I prompted her, though she seemed inwardly distressed.

Finally her eyes met mine.

'All right, I will tell you Miss Reinhart. I had always intended to. I have wanted to confess, but you see it is very hard for an old woman like me to confess to something so terrible after having tried so many years to live with my actions.'

'I must know the truth,' I encouraged her.

'I understand. It was I who took your sister's life,' she said quietly.

My mouth fell open and I shook my head with disbelief.

'You murdered her? How could you do that? She was only six years of age?' I felt anger rise in my chest and suppressed a sudden urge to scream.

Tears fell to her lap and she dabbed at her eyes.

'I did not wish for Leah or your sister to suffer any longer. Yes, I was a wretched and badly behaved girl, that is true, but in my mind I felt that I was committing an act of mercy.'

I realised that I had taken hold of either side of my chair tightly and tried to relax my grip. 'What happened that night, please tell me the entire event?'

'It was so terrible. Pixie refused to eat when Leah left the orphanage to live with her father. We all thought she would never return again and Pixie trusted no-one else. Sister Ernestine had very little patience and was somewhat cruel to her. She would bruise the girl roughly trying to force her to eat or to sit up straight. And she covered those up with a tightly wrapped shawl. It was difficult to tell how much of it was Sister and how much of it was Pixie because she would rock in her cot for hours throwing herself against the bed in a rage from time to time.

'Quite unexpectedly Leah returned to the orphanage after a few weeks, spending many hours trying to atone for her absence, but what they had developed together seemed to have been destroyed. Pixie now felt too abandoned to trust anyone ever again. She had lost too many people that she loved.

'I tried to encourage Leah to move forward with her life, to accompany me to the village dance.'

'I read about that incident in the diary,' I cut in.

'Yes, I admit I was a little envious, about the way she wanted to be with Pixie each day and then write about her every night. I had no true friends you see. Most pitied me. After Jack left and I lost the baby I fell from grace. My family and friends wanted little to do with me and Leah was the only person who visited me in the hospice. No-one else cared at all about my feelings when my baby was lost.'

She paused to look down at her lap.

'Miss Reinhart, your sister had only ever responded to Leah, and then Leah left. It was no wonder her world crashed around her for a second time. Losing her family, and then losing…'

I let out a small cry.

'I should say no more Miss Reinhart. It is too much for you.'

'Please don't stop,' I told her.

I had to hear the words, no matter the pain it caused.

'I had experienced loss myself so I knew what that was like. Ending Pixie's pain was not a decision made over a long period of time. You must believe me in that regard. I sneaked the diary out from beneath Leah's mattress which certainly improved my reading skills, but after one entry she made I had been able to decipher something else I found in it...'

She pointed at the diary. 'There was a picture of a young boy beside a grave.'

'You mean the torn book illustration?'

'Yes, but not just that, it was what Leah wrote too. She said that Pixie pointed to the grave many times.'

I nodded. 'But I think Leah did not quite understand the fixation my sister had with the picture.'

'No, she did not but I understood the picture, Miss Reinhart. Pixie had known she was never going to be loved properly, never going to grow up as a normal young lady should. She had learned quite tragically that people you love and those that love you in return do not always remain by your side. Others can take them away from you. Just like that without a warning. I tell you that I firmly believed that she held on to that page because she wished to die.'

'Oh my lord in heaven,' I said. 'Could she not have held on to it because she lost her mother? Our mother? Perhaps she saw herself in that picture. Already deceased and my mother and I mourning beside her grave.'

Miss Wakefield shook her head sadly.

'That is possible. I did not know she had a twin sister still alive and living in London. But you must believe that it tore me apart to end her life,' she said with more tears brimming in her eyes.

'How did you do it?' I pressed the handkerchief to my own eyes.

'I crept into her room late at night after everyone had retired to their beds. She was sound asleep and I stopped her breath by placing a pillow over her face. I then placed one of the small stones she used to collect inside her throat to make it appear that she choked on it. As I did so I prayed that the angels would quickly take her up to heaven.

'I knew that Leah often feared thoughts of her being sent to an asylum, but she would never have had the courage to do anything to stop it. So you must believe me when I tell you that your sister felt nothing at all because she passed away in her sleep. It happened so quickly and peacefully.'

'And what about the record of a small object lodged in her throat?'

'I placed it there to make it appear as though she had choked.'

'Did you also place the blame for her death on Leah?' I said, feeling anger rise within me.

'No! Leah could not be blamed. The key to Pixie's room had already been taken from her.

Leah instantly suspected Sister Ernestine but I always knew where the spare keys were kept. I used them often to gain entry and exit to the building.

'Miss Reinhart, I confess it was a dreadful act and I only pray the Lord forgives me, but Leah was able to move away and find work and I hoped that perhaps she might have someday married too. My desire was that she would no longer have had to wonder about your sister's fate or whether she had been given fair treatment.

'As it came about, Leah too succumbed to an illness for I have seen that she is laid to rest there in the graveyard close to Pixie herself.'

'But you *murdered* my sister!' I responded, her words falling past my ears as I stood to my feet, suddenly blinded by fury.

'You had no right to interfere in the natural order of things. It is a crime against another human being and against God Himself. Such a terrible act of injustice, and to keep the truth hidden for twenty-five years! Really! How could you?'

'Please Miss Reinhart... try to understand my reasoning.'

I hurried away from the room collecting my coat from the hallway. I could not bear to be in her home any longer. Part of me had understood her reasoning but it did not change the fact that I was repulsed by the turn of events, and even more so that she was never discovered or made accountable for her actions.

But was it too late to seek justice for Pixie?

Miss Jeannie Wakefield was a middle-aged woman who looked much older than her years. She resided alone and was a person with few friends and to be pitied.

I reached the end of the lane shaking, realising then that the diary was still sitting on her coffee table. I howled into the chilly air and leaned awkwardly against a fence. I could not bear in that moment to return inside to retrieve it. There I waited for my driver to return, and during that time wiped many a tear from my eye though I calmed myself enough to appear composed when a middle aged man sauntered past with two obedient farm dogs.

'Morning Madam.' He tipped his hat and eyed me queerly.

I felt exposed and foolish as I briefly acknowledged him then averted my gaze, sending him a clear message that I did not wish to indulge in any pleasantries, for a dishevelled woman in a fashionable dress and silk stockings standing at the edge of a field must have been a frightfully amusing sight.

Finally, when my driver arrived I ascended the carriage and wept throughout the entire journey home. I would tell Matthew everything. I would spill the whole truth.

Thirty-Three

Annie

I sat close to Mother. Her breathing had been labouring all day according to Bessie and she was unresponsive. She could barely move or speak and I knew that her mind was in some other place for much of the time.

Looking at her now, I realised that we had grown closer in the last few weeks of her life. More so than we had ever been.

Now that my search for the truth had ended, I returned to her and told her delightful stories about Pixie and she listened quietly, though she had been subdued with medication for much of the time, I knew that she heard and appreciated my words for she would lightly squeeze my hand now and then, and her eyes would smile beneath their half closed lids.

Through my voice I filled the gap of those lost years. She learned of Pixie's love of collecting small stones as Leah strolled with her through the orphanage grounds. She also learned of Pixie's affectionate nature, her courage, and her strengths. How she loved to be read to and sang to, and how the circus was a place of wonderment and one of the happiest days of her life.

I would purposely leave away any information that might distress her. Gradually my words soothed her spirit, bringing back the love that she truly felt she had lost for her daughter. A love that I knew she desperately wanted to feel again but had been too angry with herself to release.

Her head rested on the pillow, eyes fully closed.

Matthew sat outside in the waiting area. He had travelled back on the first train he could acquire a ticket for upon hearing that my Mother had once again succumbed to a stroke.

This time, however, the prognosis was bleak and the physician said she was now in God's hands and only He could decide her fate. We all feared the worst for she had refused food for more than four days and could barely keep fluids down.

I stared at her face and her bony chest rising and falling delicately as her life began slipping away, reminding me of some little bird that had fallen from its nest and tumbled to the ground.

Just after six pm in the early evening she stirred, her eyelids slowly parted. She tried to gain a little focus on her surroundings. I leaned forward and touched her cheek.

'Mother, it is me, Annie.'

She looked at me through half lidded eyes and I saw love there for the briefest moment.

The doctor arrived to check her pulse and told us to prepare ourselves. We gathered around as she beckoned with one hand. She looked at me a little anxiously. She was begging my forgiveness still, and I gently pressed my lips to her forehead and placed a kiss there.

I realised in that moment that it was not Pixie that Mother had resented and tried to avoid all these years.

It was herself.

'Mother, I want you to know that I forgive you and when you see Pixie, I wish you to tell her that I love her.'

She gave a faint nod and moved her lips. I saw that she wanted to speak but her voice was barely a whisper. I leaned closer to her face which seemed somehow bathed in a more youthful glow.

'Pixie is calling me and your father is there too.'

I began to cry upon hearing this. Matthew placed his hand on my shoulder and Bessie drew the curtains and stood at the foot of the bed with her head lowered and her hands clasped together.

I stroked Mother's hand and watched her slip away from the world. I watched her face for a long time knowing that as she came upon her last hour she was finally at peace.

Mother had been released from her pain, forgiven and was truly loved.

Pixie and my father had come to take her home.

Epilogue

June 1908

I forgave her for ending my sister's life.

It was harder than forgiving my own mother because I felt strongly about the way a person should be allowed to die, and so I could not bring myself to speak with her again.

Surprisingly, Leah's diary was mailed back to me shortly after my visit to Lowcroft Cottage and for that I could have thanked her, but I did not. I later found that there were new words scribbled in ink at the very back, which she must have added herself before returning the diary to me.

Let all that you do be done in love

Corinthians 16:13

Jeannie Wakefield died naturally in her sleep fifteen months after she had confessed her terrible deed to me. I did not attend the wake or the funeral service though I sent on a small wreath expressing my condolences. I held no lasting anger or remorse over her actions, for I had lived many years bearing a certain heaviness of sadness that I wished to be free of.

There were days when I felt at peace with my mother and at other times I still wished to scream at her in anger. I suppose I will continue to carry the guilt of having imposed upon her the disappointment of a resentful and distant child for over twenty five years.

I would also continue to carry anger at my Father over his secretive visits to Pixie, even though I understood why he could never bring her home. I always held the assumption that my mother could not live with a daughter she had broken, but mostly it was because my mother could not live with *herself*.

Matthew and I provided Pixie with a proper burial service and laid her remains next to my parents in the graveyard at St Vincent's Church.

I selected a beautiful marble headstone with a carved white stone angel sitting above it. The cherub sat with her legs crossed and her face resting in her hands. It was very much like the way Pixie once sat, crossing and re-crossing her legs with her chin pressed into both palms sulkily, preferring to be dancing or running than listening to Miss Tilda's lessons.

But I could let go of all my inner torment now. All my doubts had finally blown away with the wind that carried the seeds of truth. My family were re-united in a heavenly light filled only with love.

As for Matthew and I, we married seven months after Mother passed away. It was Christmastime and we moved into a new home together where I gave birth to our own little blessing one year later.

We named her Pixie Scarlet Leah Harvington.

Her father dotes on her and, in turn, he tells all our acquaintances that I could not possibly be a more devoted mother. Together we visit the graves of my parents and my sibling, and we always carry pure white flowers and place them on the graves.

Occasionally I take a trip with Pixie to the orphanage where she enjoys collecting the fallen leaves and placing a small mound of them on Leah's grave.

Beyond Leah Cunningham's life at the orphanage I would never know, and I felt I had no need to. I simply replaced her rotting wooden cross with a more fitting and dignified headstone. She was never known to me in person, but I felt I had grown to know and love her, and I would always owe her my fullest gratitude.

Leah's diary now rests in the Greenwich chapel in the safe care of the clergy there. It will remain there until Pixie is of an age where she can take it, if she wishes.

The only surviving legacy of her aunt.

My sister.

Pixie Amelia Reinhart.

Author's Note

There is never any easy way to write a story. To complete a book one must give up their time, expectations, and above all, self- doubt.

By giving up the latter the book will be finished.

Girl Forgotten began as a seed of an idea when I explored the idea of losing a twin. If one can imagine the strength of an invisible connection between siblings, then a *twin* sister must provide an even deeper and unbreakable bond.

I began to craft the story with that single thought in mind whilst the rest of the characters each stepped on to the stage to fill my pages with their voices. They each turned up to unfold their dreams and desires creating happiness, pain, laughter and tears, showing me the agonisingly beautiful and crushing experiences that touch us all in different ways in our day to day lives.

I'd like to thank my friends and family for their kindness and support, and I am extremely grateful to the universe for the ability to dream, plot, and plan my thoughts into the magnitude of such a thing as a book.

And lastly, I'd like to thank you, the reader, for not only choosing my novel but joining me on this writing journey. Please take a moment to write a few words on Amazon or GoodReads, for which I'd be eternally grateful.

More by the same author…

THE LAST GIFT

An Amazon No 1 Kindle best seller

> "Ripped from Dickens-era headlines, this Victorian potboiler is full of twists, turns and unexpected developments." -
>
> Writers Digest e-book Awards 2015

The Last Gift - Chapter 1

I jumped in alarm as my mother cried out. 'Don't worry, love,' my grandmother said, placing her sewing to one side. 'It's just the baby in your mother's tummy making itself known. Come on Maggie, let's get your mother a cup of tea.'

Mother smiled gratefully and Grandmama hobbled over to our little fire using her walking stick. 'I'm so tired Edith, maybe I'll just finish this shawl off then lie down,' she said.

After the tea was made she returned to her sewing, pulling me close to her side. Her knobbly, twisted hands spun into action and I watched with interest as the shawl grew longer. Both of them had been sitting beside me for hours making new clothes for the baby, and the air of excitement in the house made us all tingle.

'Ma, you should rest now and take Maggie to bed with you,' my mother said.

My grandmother and I always slept together on an old shoddy mattress as there wasn't much room in our cramped sleeping quarters. I never complained as I lay there nestled against her familiar warmth for we were often cold, having only torn pieces of cloth and paper covering the many cracks in the walls.

Grandmama fell into a deep slumber that night, but in the morning she did not awaken. My mother screamed as she shook the lifeless body which lay beside me and Father came rushing into the room in alarm. He then left the house and did not return for some time.

Mother dragged me from the bed and sat me in a chair then rushed to the window and drew the curtains. On the mirror she lay a black veil, telling me that Grandmama's spirit must not see its own reflection and become trapped within the glass.

I sat on the chair hugging my doll and stared at Grandmama lying on the bed. She appeared as if she were still asleep, the only difference being the way her white-knuckled hands had stiffened into a claw-like pose and the stench of death permeating the room.

That afternoon Father arrived with two men. They placed my grandmother's frail body inside a thin wooden box and carried her outside into the pouring rain. My parents could not afford a funeral or burial plot and so Grandmama joined the diseased bodies in the paupers grave.

My mother spent the rest of that day weeping in her chair, wooden rosary beads wrapped tightly around her fingers and draping over her extended abdomen. During the dark days to follow she sat alone by the fire, finishing off the tiny patches of clothes which became dampened with her tears.

Two days later Father and I were shocked to find Mother deliver two tiny babies, but the midwife confirmed that neither had been born with breath in their lungs. They too were placed in a little box beside Grandmama.

Later that same evening Mother packed the tiny items of clothing into a tatty worn box and Father tenderly laid his arm across her shoulders. 'It's not your fault Edith, don't blame yourself.' he said. She looked away and faced the wall to weep inconsolably over the box for many hours. Eventually, Father pried it from her tight grip and sent it away to the Sisters of Charity.

I was six years old when these tragic events befell my family in Bethnal Green, East London. From that day on my mother withdrew from reality, and instead of busying her hands making pretty gowns for Miss Charlotte at Holbrook Hall, she indulged quietly in prayer.

Carla Acheson

The Whitechapel Virgin

"Acheson has a gift for being able to bring the grit of poverty to life." -

Historical Novel Society.Org

The Whitechapel Virgin - Chapter 1

The gentleman looked down at the young girl who had tripped before him and lay sprawled on the ground with one thigh exposed.

'Young miss, are you all right?'

She glanced up at the dark-clothed stranger apprehensively before taking hold of the black-gloved hand he offered her in assistance.

'Thank you kind sir,' she replied, rising to her feet.

He studied her with interest, narrowing his eyes to examine her features beneath the yellow hue cast from the lantern above, taking particular interest in her almond-shaped eyes.

Lowering his gaze, the threadbare fabric of her clothing indicated an obvious sign of poverty right down to the scuffed dirty boots. Though if such shabby attire were to be discarded, standing before him would be a thing of innocent beauty and her sudden appearance served only to arouse his interest further. He examined the swell of her bosom where he might instinctively fathom her age, and by its relative flatness deduced that she was still at the cusp of womanhood which served only to arouse his interest further.

Discovering a young lady carrying a case along the dangerous streets of Whitechapel at such a late hour could only signify that she was either a runaway or a fallen woman caught between lodgings.

Of that he had no doubt.

He ought to know, he had spent his entire life residing amongst these women who sought their best custom late at night when gentlemen exited the many drinking establishments more than mildly intoxicated. He recognised their mischievous scent, the dubious expressions, doubtful eyes and that invisible aura of desperation they each carried upon their person. It was the latter which drove these women behind the gloomiest alleyways or beneath the sheets of unfamiliar beds.

The girl had begun trembling now, fearful eyes ringed with dark shadows darted left and right as if she were lost or confused. For which direction she were headed it appeared that she could not decide.

'Are you all right?' he questioned her again.

'Yes sir, I am looking for...' her words trailed off at the appearance of a brawling gang of youths who were exiting a tavern a short distance away. A bell rang above the door, and the girl swept her eyes to the location and kept them focused there.

'I beg your pardon, sir, but I must move on,' she told him, and began to walk away before he could raise any objection or delay her.

He nodded, tipped his hat and allowed her to proceed.

There would be no point in bothering the girl with questions, he thought to himself. It was likely that she was fleeing from a troublesome customer, the very ones who in all respects either refused to pay their dues or requested more from these girls than they were willing to provide.

He watched her approach the tavern, partly to satisfy his own curiosity, and partly to ensure her safety on the last few steps of her journey. There were more than a few offbeat characters about at this ungodly hour, for he had encountered more than a few himself over the years when roaming the narrow streets by twilight.

He watched the girl open the door, sensing fear and uncertainty in her movements. She appeared completely unfamiliar with the popular haunt. Had she paused to enquire of him, he would have warned her that inside the Boars Tavern she might find many fallen women, for this particular district alone was heaving with them.

He could also, if one insisted, describe his most favourite *belles-de-nuit* in full and accurate detail. The pallid tinge of their skin, the promiscuous display of soft flesh above their bodices, the sanguine pout of their lips.

Particularly tantalising to him was the more costly and better fed class of whore. Much more difficult to locate, but these particular ladies wore playful expressions as they peeled away layer upon layer of frilly apparel and under-garments. It was an act often repeated by twilight, and many of them, by his own conclusion, offered an exemplary standard of service.

Of course, there were also the highly personal details of his interactions with them that he could not reveal quite so openly.

And these he saved for his diary.

They were the sort of scandalous details he had convinced himself to be bright modern musings for a man of his time.

One day he, Edward Cross, would make certain that his hobby-by-description procured some extreme wealth. Well, that is, once he had found a way to debunk society's unnecessary and old-fashioned scorn of the female naked body.

Yes, the day would come when he would make that act popular again, *pleasures of the flesh*. He would bring it back into the fashion, just as "Harris' List," had done in the past with its well-documented and highly sought after list of 'Covent Garden' whores.

It was only a matter of time before his publication would tear down the veils of prudery to excite and delight men throughout the country. Men such as - well him of course. A middle class gentleman with charm, intelligence and ambition.

And what of this lovely new handsome wench?

He began to whistle a popular tune as he continued along the uneven cobbled path, the fog thickening around him.

He cast a quick glance over his shoulder to see that the girl had long since disappeared inside the tavern. Best to trouble her no further then, though he would certainly keep her in mind. Perhaps he might even pay a visit to the brewery shortly, for it was possible that the girl was '*virgen in tactus*' and in the Whitechapel district of London, those untainted gems were becoming harder and harder to find.

ABOUT THE AUTHOR

Carla lives in the UK and has worked as a book-reviewer, having interviewed and published book reviews and articles for best-selling and award-winning authors.

Her articles and reviews have been featured in various publications, as well as Waterstones Quarterly UK Magazine. Other novels are, 'The Whitechapel Virgin,' and 'The Last Gift,' which became a Kindle Bestseller in 2015.

New editions of all titles have been published by Charlotte Greene, Dorset, England.

Connect with the author on the following social media links:

Official website: www.carla-acheson.com
Facebook: https://www.facebook.com/achesonbooks/
Twitter: @Carla_Anne

Printed in Great Britain
by Amazon